The Girls Love the Boys in the Band

by

June Bug

PublishAmerica
Baltimore

ISBN: 1-60703-201-5
PUBLISHED BY PUBLISHAMERICA, LLLP
www.publishamerica.com
Baltimore

Printed in the United States of America

I would like to dedicate this book to the love of my life, Robert Antjuan Curry. Because of you, I have discovered my true passion, writing. You brought something out of me that I didn't even know existed, and I thank you for being such a big influence on my life. Whether we are together or apart, I will always love you, and I will never forget the things I have learned during the course of our relationship. With you, I have grown into the woman I am today. Once again, thank you.

Love always,

June Bug

Acknowledgements

First and foremost, I would like to thank God who is ahead of my life. He blessed me with the talent to write. So, I give him all the honor. I would also like to thank my my family and friends for being so supportive. I truly appreciate it. I would also like to thank my fans for believing me, and giving me the encouragement to share my gift with you all. Of course, I would like to thank Mr. Curry again, for being such an influence on me. God definitely put you in my life for a reason.

Thanks again,
June

Introduction

You know it's funny how people want to get closer to God when something tragic happens in their life. I hate to put myself in that category of people; however, it is what it is. I have never prayed so hard, and I have never cried so loud until now. I feel weak because I am very aware of what's going on, but God has been the only one getting me through the storm. This experience has most definitely been the most complicated experience I have ever had in my life; but I will not get discouraged. God wouldn't put me through anything that I couldn't overcome.

I know that I can't shake the man that I love so dearly as if he were a man I met yesterday. To be honest, I am not trying to. I believe that he needs me now more than ever. Although it may seem like he doesn't realize my true feelings yet, doesn't mean that he never will. I sincerely believe that we are meant to be. God placed him in my life not only to bring me closer to him, but to show me love, true love, and everything that comes along with it. I am a living testimony. I'm here to tell my story about how God can change what may seem to be the unchangeable.

Chapter 1
Hello, Love

I was 17 years old when I met the love of my life, Robert Antjuan Curry. It was September 3, 2003, his birthday to be exact. I remember it like it was yesterday. It just so happened, that I was there visiting a mutual friend, which happened to be the guy I was kickin it with at the time being. His name was Deandre. Robert and Deandre were long time best friends. They met when they were kids after being randomly selected to be in a group together. After the group had disbursed, they continued to pursue their friendship, and had been inseparable ever since. Deandre introduced Robert to me as Antjuan. Only his family called him Robert. I didn't even discover his name was really Robert until further into our friendship.

Deandre and I kicked it periodically because he was always on the go, in and out of town. He never really gave me enough time to get too attached. However, I still had mad feelings for him. He had a swag that went with his personality that made him extremely attractive. When he introduced Antjuan and me to each other, I didn't really pay too much attention to him. He was there with his girlfriend Shanda, and I was there with Deandre. I had no reason to be showing him any attention…but who knew what was to come of us in the future.

Antjuan and Deandre had eventually moved to New Jersey to work with multi-platinum recording artist, Wyclef. At first, I was upset that Deandre left, but after time passed I was more than okay with his decision to focus on his career. I had started to kick it with a few random guys, but none of them really tickled my fancy.

One day, after my friend Jamie's open house, me and a couple of my girls wanted to find something to get into. Detroit didn't have that much to offer the people in my age bracket though. Half of us were too young to do anything. So, after pondering for a while, we all decided to just go downtown and ride around. To my surprise, downtown was jumpin'. I had totally forgotten that Eminem and 50 cent had a concert. By the time we had arrived down there, the concert had just ended, which meant, niggas and bitches everywhere!

After turning down every guy that approached me that night, I finally got approached by the right one. He was fine as hell, with a body more cut than an ice sculpture, and had a tone so fuckin' sexy that when he spoke he made my panties moist.

"Excuse me ma, can I talk to you for a second?" His deep, sexy, intriguing voice began to send chills through my spine. Even though I was interested, I played it cool, and thought it would be kind of fun to play hard to get.

"Can you?" I said. "There's not much you can say in a second, but we can see what you can get out." He laughed at my sarcasm. He saw right through me though. He knew he was fine as hell, and it didn't take much for me for me to give him some play.

"I just wanted to know if I can get to know you. You are very attractive," he said.

"We can probably work something out…but before we continue conversing, what's your name?

"Antonio."

"Well Antonio, I am June. It's a pleasure to meet you."

"The pleasure's all mine," he said grinning, showing off his pearly whites.

Antonio wasn't alone. He had a friend for each one of my girls. Delvon, which was Antonio's brother, got with my girl Felicia. Antonio's best friend, Mark, got with my girl Brittany. Last, but certainly not least, Alanzo, Delvon's best friend, got with my girl Jamie. It didn't take long at all for Jamie and Alanzo to hit it off. About five minutes after hello, Antonio and I found them two making out in the front seat of his car.

"Now before you go thinking that I am anything like my girl, let's get the record straight. I'm not!" I told him offensively.

"I never said you were, and neither did I give you the impression that I thought you were." He replied.

"True...but you know what they say...birds of a feather, flock together."

He laughed. "Not necessarily. I roll with a lot of niggas that do shit I wouldn't do everyday."

I elaborated on how I thought it was unladylike for her to be letting this nigga suck on her titties, and she barely knew his name. Anyone could have walked or drove by and saw that. I definitely didn't want Antonio to think that I was a fast ass like her.

After exchanging conversation for most of the night, we finally exchanged numbers. We talked everyday. He definitely had my attention. Not only was he fine as hell, but he was also funny. I never knew how attractive it was for a man to be humorous, until I met him. When we finally saw each other again, it was a wrap! He should have never come over looking and smelling as good as he did. I wanted him so bad; I didn't care how I got him. There wasn't anything special about it. We did it right then and there, in the back seat of his car, on the fourth level in a parking garage. We had no shame. I had never done anything as spontaneous as that in my life. I couldn't believe after I had just given him that long ass speech about how I thought it was unladylike for my girl to do what she did, I turned around and banged this nigga a week later. There was just something daring about Antonio that brought out a side of me that I didn't even know existed.

Being with Antonio became a routine. The sex was good. So, going elsewhere was most definitely not an option. We saw each other damn near everyday. Then, on one particular day I asked him to come see me, but he was unavailable.

"You must have some other chick to hook up with today." I said jokingly.

"Not at all," he chuckled.

"So what's the deal? I really want to see you today."

"I'm on my way to the hospital. My daughter is about to be born."

Immediately I laughed because I thought he was joking. Antonio didn't have any kids, or at least to my knowledge. He instantaneously stopped me and questioned my laughter. That's when I knew he was serious. The only thing that was running through my mind at that moment was, *How the fuck is this nigga on his way to the hospital to await his daughter's birth that I knew nothing about.* I felt like he should have been man enough and said something from the door instead of withholding that from me.

I couldn't fake the funk no longer than I already had, so I approached the situation that was at hand.

"So, why the hell didn't you tell me that you had a daughter on the way when I met you?" I said angrily.

"What the hell are you talking about? I did tell you!" He snapped back.

When he said that, I suddenly paused and tried to replay that conversation in my head, but nothing came up. Then he said something that triggered me to remember us conversing about if he had kids or not.

"You asked me did I have any kids, and I told you no…but I have one on the way."

I had no idea that he was serious, because after he said that, he laughed hysterically and so did I. I thought he was joking, but that damn sure wasn't a joke. It was a situation that I was uncomfortable being in.

Antonio had my head all messed up. If I would have known that he had a daughter on the way, I probably wouldn't have given him the time of day. I felt like I was too young to be getting involved with a nigga who had a baby. After all, I was only 17. While I was sitting at home trippin', I felt like I needed to talk to my girls. When I called them and told them what happened, half of them seemed to be shocked. The other half wasn't shocked at all. They even elaborated on how they thought he was a hoe anyway. I gave him the benefit of the doubt though. *Just because he had a daughter on the way, didn't mean he was out fucking around he made a mistake,* I told myself. I really didn't know what the truth was. I just didn't want to make any assumptions either.

After Antonio's daughter was born, to my surprise, he came over. He tried to make me feel secure with the fact that just because he had a daughter, didn't mean that we couldn't pursue anything. He even tried to make it abundantly clear that he and his baby mama was no longer together, and that they didn't get along. He also said that getting her pregnant wasn't deliberate, but he took the responsibility as a man and accepted God's plan. I figured, if what he was telling me was the truth, what's the worst that could happen?

The worst that could happen, happened not too long after I found out he had a child. It's funny how everything seems so cool in the beginning of a relationship, and then as time goes by, the shit starts to hit the fan. One day, out the clear blue sky after Antonio and I had a date at the movies, I noticed that he was acting really strange. I kept asking him what was wrong, but he insisted on telling me later. He dropped me off after what had seemed to be a nice date. Then, twenty minutes later, I got the call. From the sound of his voice, I knew that what he had to say wasn't going to be good.

"So, what's the matter baby?" I asked.

"I don't know how to tell you this."

"Tell me what?"

"What I'm about to tell you."

My heart was beating expeditiously, and my words and hands began to tremble. I tried to put myself at ease by telling myself, "Maybe it's not that bad." At first, he procrastinated and told me how much he liked me. Then he elaborated about how bad he felt about the news he was about to tell me. I was beginning to run out of patience. Then, that's when he hit me with it.

"I have another girlfriend."

"What! Why the hell did you even pursue me then? First you tell me you gotta baby on the way, but I still chose to fuck with you. Now you are telling me that you don't only have a child, but you have another girlfriend. Wow! Fuckin Niggas!"

"I'm sorry."

"You're sorry," I said furiously. "Sorry for what…wasting my time?"

"I really like you though."

"Sure you do Antonio, I can tell."

He told me that he had been dealing with her since I met him. In a nut shell, he was tired of being a dog, and he wanted to do the right thing. I really didn't have too much to say after that. I just hung up the phone with disappointment and disbelief. How could I have been so naive?

After we disconnected, I called my girl Felicia over to the house and told her what happened.

"I can't believe this hoe ass nigga got a fuckin girlfriend! This nigga was spending damn near every night with me. Where the fuck was she? When did he have time to see her?"

"Well, a nigga don't need a lot of time to fuck around. When he wasn't with you, he was probably with her."

"That just foul then!"

"Niggas are foul! They do shit like that all the fuckin time. At least he told you instead of you catching him up in some bullshit."

"Well that nigga should have been honest from the jump! If I still wanted to fuck with him after knowing all of that, at least it would have been a decision I made for myself."

"If he would have, you probably wouldn't have messed with him."

"True…but he didn't know if I would or wouldn't have. There are girls that don't give a fuck. He should have let me make tat decision for myself."

"Well, there is no need to get all worked up over that hoe ass nigga. Trust me, it's not worth your tears. There are plenty of other niggas out here. No need to sweat this one."

Even though she was right, there was something inside of me that yearned for answers to all the questions running through my head. Later that night, I waited for my parents to go to sleep so I could steal my mom's car to go talk to him face to face. I went over there without any warning. I didn't want to give him any room to give me any excuses as of why he couldn't see me. When I pulled up, he was outside sitting on the porch, with this real fucked up look on his face. I was never the type to just pop up at a nigga house, but I thought it was the best thing to do at the time.

I had rehearsed in my mind all of the questions I wanted to ask him. So when I began to talk, it just flowed right out. His responses were pretty wack though. For most of the questions I asked, he gave me "I don't know" answers. I felt like I was wasting my time. As the time approached for my departure, he kept telling me how sorry he was for hurting me. By that time, everything he said had sounded like a bunch of bullshit. So, to avoid from getting any more pissed off than I already was, I just hopped in the car and drove off with no intentions of ever going back.

It didn't take too long for me to start feeling lonely. Since I was so comfortable with Antonio, I figured that it was okay to get a fix every now and then. I should have known that was a bad idea though. Eventually my feelings were wrapped in him again, and I was in the same position I was in the beginning. This time, when Antonio and I had started kickin' it, I found out more than I could handle.

I finally discovered who the girlfriend was that he was with when we first broke it off. I was a fool to think that he had left her alone. I didn't even ask if it was over before I decided to talk back to him. I just assumed that it was over. I must say, I was rather disgusted when I figured out who she was. Her name was Ayanna. Not only was she fifteen years older than him, which made her about 36, but she also had six kids. Her oldest son was a couple of years younger than Antonio. I couldn't help but wonder, "What the hell is wrong with this Bitch?" The saddest part about the situation was, I saw her plenty of times before, but not once did I think that she was anything remotely close to being his woman. If I recall correctly, he had me under the impression that she was his sister. I didn't think not to believe him. When we were around each other, she didn't act anything like his woman.

I tried to make myself understand, "Why the hell was he fucking around with that old ass bitch with six kids anyway?" It was evident though. She bought him everything he wanted, such as: phones, shoes, clothes, cars, etc. You named it, he got it. She was most definitely a fool in love. She knew everything he was doing. She just didn't care enough to leave him alone. He depended on her and that was enough to get her through the day.

After I discovered he was still fucking around with Ayanna, I found out he was fucking damn near everyone. He was a savage. After a while, I couldn't take it anymore. I decided to really fall back. This time I was I was more than confident I didn't want to go back. He wasn't good for me. We still saw each other though, because Delvon, Alanzo, and I had become really close friends. I even took it as far as labeling them as my best friends.

For comfort, I went to my friend Tyrone, and told him all about my troubles with Antonio. He and his girl were going through problems similar to mine, except the roles were reversed and she was the one cheating. One day when I was on the phone with him, something I said triggered him to remember that he knew exactly who Antonio was.

"What kind of car does Antonio drive?"

"A Sebring…Why?"

"Does it have a lot of artwork on it?"

"Oh Lord…yeah."

"Man, that's the same nigga that go with my girl Tiana?"

"Tiana? I haven't heard that name before. That nigga is a trip. How many fucking girlfriends do this nigga got?"

"You know, it's funny because the whole time you were describing him, I was thinking it may be him. The more you talked about him. The more I realized it was."

I found it very ironic that one of the girls that Antonio was playing me with was one of Tyrone's friends. When Antonio had found out that Tyrone confided in me and told me that he was playing me with her, he was infuriated.

"That nigga just mad cause his girl fucking around on him!" Antonio blurted.

"How would you know what his girl is doing? Are you fuckin her?"

"No, but Delvon is. She be coming over her all the time getting the brakes knocked off her ass."

"Are you serious?"

"Hell yeah! Not only that, but I was fucking the girl he was in love with before her."

"Oh my God! Are you talking about…"

"Latriece!" he said, cutting me off. " The first time I fucked her was in the bathroom at our job. That nigga just mad, and hating like a motherfucka."

"How can you really get mad at him for telling me though? He is my friend, not yours."

"That's true, but I just don't like when niggas stick they nose in business that doesn't concern them."

I couldn't believe all the stuff that Antonio had told me. It was a big Jerry Springer mess. I felt bad having to tell Tyrone all that I knew, but I felt like I had to. I wasn't about to have him fucking around with this bitch that was fucking around on him. After I told him, he was in disbelief, and very hurt about the news I had broke to him. He informed me that he was just about to buy her a truck for her birthday. I sure was glad I caught him before he did that. Even though, he was grateful that I had told him everything. He didn't know how to approach the situation. He said he needed some time to think.

The next day, me and my girls were shopping around at Fairlane Mall, and I decided to stop in the store I knew she worked at. When she saw me, she greeted me as she usually would. Then, I politely I asked her to step to the back so we could talk for a second.

"So, how are things going with you and Tyrone?" I asked.

"Things are great! Couldn't be better!"

"Really? You know Tyrone is like one of best friends?"

"Yeah, I know."

"But I bet you don't know who else is like a best friend to me."

"Who?"

"Delvon." When I said his name, her eyes got big ass hell. She knew right then and there that she was caught up in some bullshit.

"Delvon who?" She asked, trying to throw me off.

"Denisha, cut the bullshit! You know who I am talking about. I'mma tell you like this, Tyrone is my nigga…and I am not going to allow you to be fucking around on him like that. I know about the Delvon shit. You know I know…otherwise I wouldn't even be talking to about this shit right now. If you love Tyrone, then you better start acting like it, cause that nigga loves you. I don't want to have to hurt you. So, get your shit together. If you don't, this won't be the last time you see me. Next time, I will be doing less talking."

Denisha didn't say anything to Tyrone about me threatening her. I knew she wouldn't. She didn't want to get caught up in any bullshit. Tyrone loved Denisha so much that he chose not to believe what I had told him about her and Delvon. Tyrone and I had eventually grew apart because he still wanted to be with his girl, and not listen to me. I knew that it was selfish, but I couldn't stand to watch her hurt him like that. Whenever I would see the two of them together, or even her by herself, we would get into a verbal altercation. I was very protective of his feelings. He eventually became submissive to her, and disassociated himself from me. I was more than hurt because of his decision, but there was nothing more I could do than accept the fact that he was a fool in love. He eventually moved to Atlanta, and that was the end of that.

Chapter 2
Welcome Back

It was at least six months since the last time Deandre and I had seen or talked to each other. When we spoke again, it was February 6, 2004. He randomly called me while I was over my friend Michelle's house. Michelle was my best friend that I've had since the seventh grade. I never really had a friend that was as close to me as Michelle was. There was nothing I wouldn't do for her, and in return there was nothing she wouldn't do for me. Labeling her my best friend was an understatement. She was more like my sister. When Deandre called, he asked if I would come over to see him. Lord knows how good Deandre made me feel. So, of course my reply to him was yes. When Michelle and I arrived at his house, I started to get a really uncomfortable feeling in the pit of my stomach. It was more awful than butterflies. Deandre had been gone for so long that I didn't even know how to act around him anymore. I was unsure if he had even liked me still. A lot of things were running through my head, such as: Was he still attractive? Would he think I was still attractive? Was his personality the same? I just hoped and prayed for the best. When he opened the door, he was still good looking Deandre. That took a lot of weight off my shoulders. Now all I had to do was see how Deandre felt about me.

After we exchanged hugs and I miss you's, we went to his room and conversed for a while.

"So, what do you pretty ladies have up for tonight?"

"You tell me." I replied.

"Well, my boy mama is throwing a party tonight. You are more than welcome to slide through if you don't have anything planned."

I definitely didn't mind going, because that meant I would get to spend more time with him. The decision was ultimately up to Michelle though.

"You know Michelle, you should really come. I think you might really like my boy." Deandre said, trying to persuade Michelle into saying yes.

"Yeah, I bet." Michelle replied.

Michelle wasn't the type to feed into to all of that hype. She decided to go ONLY because I wanted to go.

"So who's your friend?" I asked out of curiosity.

"You met him before. Do you remember Antjuan?"

"Kind of...but doesn't he have a girlfriend?"

The last time I checked Antjuan had a woman. So, I asked what happened. He kept it brief and said that they broke up. That was good and music to my ears, because I didn't want my best friend hooking up with anyone that was already in a relationship, and definitely no repeats of what I had been through with Antonio.

When we arrived at the party, Antjuan's mother, Lisa, greeted us at the door with two shot glasses filled with liquor ready to be guzzled. I was far from the drinking type, and so was Michelle. So, I asked if we could pass.

Lisa said, "NO! If you want to come in, you have to take a shot...Those are the rules!"

I hated liquor with a passion, but I took the shot anyway. Michelle stood her ground though on how she really didn't want it though. So, I asked her if I could just take the shot for her. Surprisingly, she said yes. I hadn't been in this party no longer than five minutes and I was already tipsy. All I could say to myself was, *What the hell did Deandre get me into?*

My memory was a little weary because I didn't really remember what Antjuan looked like. So, I asked Deandre where he was, and it was as if I had spoken him up. Like a movie, he came from around the corner in slow motion, and when I saw him my knees began to buckle. The funny thing was, he wasn't stepping outside himself to be attractive. If I recall correctly, he had on a tank top, and some jogging pants. He still looked sexy as hell to me though. He had the sexiest eyes that I'd ever seen. I couldn't understand how I managed to overlook all of his ravishing features the first time we met. I didn't even notice how long and pretty his hair was. I was aware of his braids, but I didn't know his shit was "like that". Then to top it off, he had a hell of a swagger. In just that moment I knew I was infatuated.

"Antjuan, you remember June right?" Deandre said.

"Yeah, I remember her," he said as he embraced me with a hug.

"So, how have you been?" I asked with this huge smile on my face.

"I have been good. What about yourself?" he said smiling back.

"Couldn't be better actually." I replied as I licked my lips seductively.

It was as if he had me in a trance. I couldn't keep my eyes off of him the entire time we were around each other. I even tried to cuddle up with Deandre as a distraction, but it was still very obvious that I wanted Antjuan. I kept complimenting him on how cute I thought he was, and told Michelle that she needed to get on. Michelle wasn't stupid by a long shot though. It was obvious to her that I wanted Antjuan. She saw my glow. So, she just told me that she wasn't interested.

After we chatted for a while, Antjuan's mother and a couple of her friends requested that Antjuan and Deandre entertain us by singing a song that they had wrote together . I was looking forward to this, because I loved to hear Deandre sing. To my surprise, when they started singing, I could hardly pay any attention to Deandre. When Antjuan started singing, I was suddenly captivated. I had chills running all through my whole body. I had heard a lot of people sing before, but none of them had the effect that Antjuan had on me. That's when I fell in love. As he sang his verse, I noticed I caught his eye. I felt a connection. For every word he sang, I imagined it being directed towards me. I wanted him, and there was nothing I could do to stop it. I felt something that I couldn't ignore, no matter how hard I tried… and believe me, I tried.

That night when I went home, I couldn't stop thinking about Antjuan. I kept asking myself what I was going to do about it, but nothing came to mind. It felt right, yet so wrong. To my knowledge, Deandre had never done anything to me. True enough he wasn't my man, or anything close to it, but he still didn't deserve that kind of treatment from me. I was pretty sure he was talking to other girls, but at least they weren't my friends.

The next morning I woke up from a very disturbing dream. I dreamed that I told Deandre that I was no longer interested in him, and I got with Antjuan. That dream had my head all fucked up. Later that day, I ran into my friend Shatiece. I told her about how Deandre was in town, and how he had this sexy ass friend that could sing that she might be interested in. She had a thing for R&B niggas. So, I knew that she was interested. I tried to at least hook one of my friends up with Antjuan, despite how I felt. I figured it would keep me from messing around with him. I called Deandre, and asked if he wanted to hook up. I even used his method and told him I had a girl for his boy to kick it with so he would say yes. I was right, he said yes.

The plan was to hook up with them later. I didn't know what later was for them. So, I made up my own time. Shatiece and I went over to Deandre's house, and when we arrived, we discovered he wasn't there. His aunt, who was a friend of the family, informed me that he was around the corner at Antjuan's house. Since Deandre's aunt was familiar with me, she offered me directions. Finding them wasn't as complicated as I thought it would be. When we pulled up, we could see Antjuan, Deandre, and Antjuan's sister, Marilyn, dancing through the big glass window in their living room. When Antjuan came to the door, he was shocked to see me. Deandre was shocked as well.

"How did you know we were here?" Antjuan asked when he

opened the door.

"Well, I am not stalking yall. I went to Deandre's house, and his aunt sent us here."

"You good. I was just wondering how you knew where I stayed. I'm not trippin. Come in and have a seat."

When we walked in the house, I observed how they had moved all of the furniture out of the way to rehearse for whatever they were getting prepared for. It just so happened that Shatiece and I were both dancers, so we were more than interested in what was going on.

"So, what are you practicing for?" I asked.

"We gotta show at Cass Tech in a few weeks," said Antjuan.

"Straight up! You know I dance right?"

"That's right…you sure do," said Deandre.

I thought it would be a great opportunity to get in where I fit in because dancing was my passion.

"So, do yall need anymore dancers?" I asked.

"Actually we do," said Deandre.

"If you don't mind, could you dance for us? I wanna see if you got what we are looking for."

"Certainly."

Shatiece and I had danced together often. So, we had a couple of routines in mind that we could show them. After we showed them a piece that we choreographed together. Then, we did a little something individually. Antjuan and Deandre liked what they saw, and they invited us to rehearsal that took place the next day.

After we had our so-called audition, we chilled with Deandre and Antjuan for a little while. Shatiece seemed to like Antjuan, which was supposed to be a good thing. However, there was something inside of me that was extremely jealous of her. I tried to stay cooped up with Deandre as much as he would let me . I did that to keep my mind off of Antjuan, but I wasn't doing a good job. Deandre was acting a little distant. I figured it was because I was being so obvious about liking Antjuan. Whatever it was, I knew something was wrong with him. I was just too afraid to ask.

Rehearsal began the next day as scheduled. I had my mind set to give it my all, because I wanted to make a good impression. Antjuan peeped how hard I was working, and he loved my dedication and drive. After rehearsal, Antjuan and I got a chance to have a real conversation.

"I want to thank you June for helping us out. That truly means a lot to me."

"The pleasure is all mine. I have been trying to find something like this to be apart of for a while now."

"You dance really well, and I really enjoy working with you."

"I enjoy working with you as well." I said, blushing

He tried to keep it professional, but I wanted to get personal. So, I started asking personal questions.

"So what happened with you and ummmm….what's her name?" I asked acting as if I didn't know her name, but really did.

"Who?" he replied acting as if he didn't know who I was talking about.

"I think her name was Shana." I lied.

"Oh…you mean Shanda?"

"Yeah…her."

"Shit, we broke up."

"That's it? Yall just broke up. No reason behind that?"

"Yeah, but I just don't wanna talk about it."

"I respect that."

I didn't want to spoil the conversation talking about his ex, so I changed the subject. After we conversed for about a half an hour, I realized how I wasn't paying Deandre any attention. Although Shatiece was talking to him, I knew he noticed my absence. I wasn't making myself look good to him at all. I eventually got up and tried to show him some attention, but he didn't seem like he wanted it. I knew he wasn't stupid. He was probably upset because I tried to play him for a fool. The truth was, I did like Deandre. I just couldn't control what

I felt for Antjuan. I never really was the type to go in between friends, but that damn Antjuan had a hold on me that I just couldn't shake. I needed a resolution, and I needed one fast. Was I going to try to pursue something with Deandre, or make a move on Antjuan? I was beyond befuddled. The truth of the matter was, something had to give.

Chapter 3
Getting Close

We damn near practiced everyday until show time. Antjuan and Deandre had added a few more dancers, who were friends of theirs. It was a good idea to add them because we would make the stage look fuller with more people. If I recall correctly, it was me, Shatiece, Marilyn, Bianca, Sherrie, Latriece, and Amanda. At first it seemed to be a good idea, but after I peeped game, it just turned out to be an awkward situation. Amanda and I both liked Deandre, and Bianca, Shatiece, and I liked Antjuan. Sherrie and Latriece wasn't a threat at all. They were always in their own little world, not really paying attention to either one of them. Of course, we didn't have to worry about Marilyn. Antjuan was very protective of his sister, and he wasn't having that shit even if she was interested in someone. There was only one person she could have liked anyway.

I wasn't certain if Antjuan knew how I felt about him. We had become very close friends over the last few weeks, but I would just talk to him about Deandre whenever we did talk, and got advice about what I should do. I soon found out that Deandre wasn't really feeling me like I thought he was. I didn't really understand why he wasn't though. Maybe it was because he was feeling Amanda more. I didn't know. I still tried though, because I knew he didn't always feel like that. So, I tried to win him back.

One night, rehearsal ended earlier than expected. A lot of the dancers didn't show up, and Deandre was a no show as well. My father was expecting to pick me up at least 2 hours after the original time our rehearsal was suppose to let out. So, that left Antjuan and me with a lot of time on our hands. At first, we made up this random routine together. Then, we conversed for a while. We talked about Deandre as usual, but after a while, I got tired of talking about him. So, I changed the subject to Shatiece.

"So, what's up with you and Shatiece?" I asked, hoping he would give me a bad response.

"Nothing really. She's cool, but I don't think I can trust her like that."

I cared about Antjuan. So, I just kept it real with him. I simply told him that I wouldn't trust her either. I felt bad after saying that. After all, she was my friend. There was just something about Antjuan that made me very protective of his feelings.

"So, why shouldn't I trust her?" he asked.

"Well, she just talks to a lot of dudes. I don't think she is someone that you should be trying to pursue a relationship with."

After that statement, I really felt like I was just plain hating on the girl. I wasn't doing it deliberately. He just had me so gone to the point that I forgot who was my friend first.

We continued conversing for an hour or so. Then, I suggested that we just chill and listen to some music. His sister had a pile of cd's next to the radio, but they were all unlabeled. So, he just randomly selected one, and let it play. We didn't notice until about four songs into the cd, that every song that had previously played was slow and sexy. The music intensified the sexual tension that I felt for Antjuan. For each song that played, I imagined him doing all the freaky things the song described. I pictured him being very good at it too. After a while, our conversation had pretty much ceased, and we were at least three feet closer than we were when we first started conversing.

As the music continued to play, my hormones began to jump out of control. I had my head resting on his chest, as we shared a recliner. Slowly but surely, I began to feel his finger tips caressing my back. Each stroke made my pussy thump. At that moment, I knew he

27

wanted what I wanted. I could see and feel his nature rising through his pants the more we made physical contact. We wanted each other bad, but we both wanted the other person to make the first move. After bullshitin' for about twenty minutes or so, we finally decided to cut the crap. Neither one of us actually made the first move. It was a mutual move. No one went before the other.

I kissed that man like I had never kissed anyone in my life. He was most definitely the best kisser I ever had. That was bad. I no longer just wanted him. I felt like I needed him inside of me. I wasn't sure if he felt like he needed me, but he damn sure wanted the pussy. During our moment, I had noticed that no man had EVER made me feel the way he did when we kissed, or touched, or when he was just simply in my presence. When he was caressing my body, I felt like I could have exploded. It got to the point where I really couldn't take it anymore.

Curiosity was knocking at my door. From the look in his eyes, curiosity had got a hold of him as well. I figured that since we already started, we might as well finish. I had intensions of fucking the shit out of him, that way he would have no choice but to come back. I began to work my way down to his pants, and right when I was about to see what he was working with, his friend Skyler busted through the door. We immediately jumped up as if we were getting caught doing something we had no business doing. The truth was, we didn't have any business doing shit. I hated the thought of Deandre finding out that Antjuan and I were fucking around through someone else, but luckily, Skyler had no idea that Deandre and I kicked it at all. So, that took a little weight off of my shoulders.

"So can I see you tomorrow?" Antjuan asked.

"Of course you can. What time do you wanna hook up?

"Early," he said in that sexy tone that I fancied so much.

"I got you baby." I replied as I kept thinking about how wet he just made my pussy.

All night, I tossed and turned because I couldn't wait to get what

I'd been craving for so long. Deandre wasn't going to hold me back from this one. As soon as I woke up, I told my father that it was imperative that I make my morning rehearsal. I exaggerated how the show was in a couple of days, and all the dancers needed to be there. He fell for it as usual. I told him any and everything I needed to in order for him to take me. When he dropped me off, I began to walk to the door, my heart began to beat really fast, and I had a stomach full of butterflies. I knocked on the door, and as I waited, I made sure everything was in place. The hair was nice, I smelled good, the gloss was poppin, and the outfit was cute. I was ready.

When the door opened, my heart dropped, and so did my face. Deandre was the one who came to the door. By that time, I didn't know what to do or think. My first thought was that Antjuan had set me up. I didn't understand. I thought the feelings we had were mutual feelings. Come to find out, Deandre came to Antjuan's house that morning just because he wanted to. It was nothing more or nothing less. Antjuan and Deandre were best friends, so it wasn't like he was going to kick him out. I just acted normal. I wasn't sure if Deandre knew about what happened between Antjuan and I, but I didn't want to be the one to give it away.

"So what are you doing here so early?" Deandre asked.

"Well, I wanted to add some choreography to the routine. It's not a problem that I am here is it?" I said, trying not to look suspicious.

"No it's not a problem at all. I am actually happy to see you."

"Really? That's a shock!" I said, with this stunned look on my face.

Lately, Deandre had been really distant, but out of all the days he wanted to show me some attention, it would be the day after me and his best friend made out. The sad thing was, I couldn't act any different. I felt like a hoe. We weren't doing much, but it felt wrong. I could feel Antjuan burning a whole in my back with his eyes as he watched us "cake". This was the first time ever that I simply wanted Deandre to just leave me alone. He wasn't all in my face, but the little attention he did show me made me feel awkward as hell.

To add to making me feel awkward as hell, Antjuan and Deandre were supposed to pick up some things that we needed for the show, and they strung me right along with them.

"Well June, since you're here, you can come with us to get some things for the show."

I looked at Antjuan, and then looked back at Deandre, and for the first time in life, I realized that I was caught up in a love triangle. I didn't know what to do. On one hand, I really liked Deandre, even though he had been showing a little lack of interest. On the other hand, Antjuan had me gone in the head. He made me feel ways no man had ever made me feel. If I would have said no, then Deandre would have known something was up. If I would have said yes, then I would have been extremely uncomfortable. I just sucked it up, and catered to the situation.

"Yeah, that's cool. I need to pick up some things for myself as well."

I tried to avoid being uncomfortable as much as possible, but that was more than impossible. I didn't even want to sit in the front seat, because I didn't feel right sitting next to either one of them. Antjuan was doing little shit like acting like he was looking in the rear view mirror to fix himself, but was really looking at me. He even had the nerve to lick those sexy ass lips at me while doing it. I couldn't handle it. So, I just looked out of the window and acted like it didn't happen. To tell the truth, I wanted to kick Deandre out of the car myself. I kept having flashbacks from the night before. I was yearning to take it to the next level.

As awkward as it was, I had a lot of fun with the both of them. They were a very entertaining pair, and I could see why they were best friends. They seemed to be really happy when they were around each other. Although I knew that what I was doing was wrong, I knew that it wasn't enough to break up their friendship. I figured Antjuan did what he did because of how he felt, not because he was a disloyal nigga.

When we arrived back at Antjuan's, Deandre came up with this bright idea.

"Hey man, I think we should have a sleepover tomorrow." Deandre said to Antjuan.

"What kind of sleepover?" Antjuan asked.

"The show is in two days, we can practice, and get fucked up. It'll be fun. Me, you, our boys, and all the dancers....Come on! You can't tell me that don't sound like fun?"

"Yeah, it does! Let's do it!" Antjuan said, sounding overly excited.

At the time, that didn't seem like such a bad idea. Then, when I went home and contemplated about it, reality hit me. The next day was going to be more than just an awkward situation with Antjuan and Deandre. I thought about what was going to happen once the lights went out, and who it was going to happen with. They both had a hell of a lot of options.

Chapter 4
Getting Closer

The day of the sleepover was a very unusual day. I definitely stepped outside of myself to fit in with everyone else. I drank, which was something I normally wouldn't do. I couldn't really get into drinking like that because my father was an alcoholic, and he almost died from it, until he got a liver transplant. I even smoked weed that night. I really wasn't a smoker. I had tried to smoke some weed a couple of times before, but I would never get high so I saw no point in doing it. Then, Antjuan taught me how to hit it right. After that, I was on cloud nine. With the liquor and weed in my system, it didn't make it hard at all to get horny. I didn't want to fuck Antjuan though, because of obvious reasons. It just wouldn't have been a good look. So, I went to see what my chances were with Deandre.

Whenever I got the chance, I would be dancing on him, kissing him on his neck, or whispering sweet nothings in his ear. It seemed like it was a go, but then he started acting really strange. Once I really started paying attention, I noticed that pretty much everyone was watching us. I really couldn't recall who Amanda was talking to, but whoever it was, I knew that she was talking about me and Deandre. She seemed to be pretty upset with what she saw. I knew that they use to kick it, but that didn't mean a damn thing to me. However, I wasn't in the mood to compete, because I felt like it was a battle that I couldn't win anyway. Deandre just wasn't interested in me like he use to be. I decided to fall back, and when I did, Amanda and Deandre were cuddled up for the remainder of the night. It was obvious to me and everyone else that I wasn't who he wanted.

I was hurt, but that was just karma biting me in the ass. I didn't let my feelings show though. I just kept it moving. As much as I wanted to be like, "Fuck it! If you don't want me, then I will just go to yo boy who do." There was something inside of me that allowed me to keep my cool. Besides, Bianca was all on Antjuan's dick for most of the night anyway. That left me and Shatiece in the same position. Shatiece didn't let that shit faze her though. When the lights went out she was laid up with somebody else.

I was very tempted to make a move on Antjuan. It didn't help that he was lying right next to me. We had exchanged a couple of feels, but all that was over when Bianca got up to go in the bedroom. He followed behind her shortly after that, and I knew exactly what that meant. I wasn't too upset though. They probably had plans to fuck with each other that night, and it was wrong for us to be fucking around anyway. I just rolled over, sexually frustrated, and took it as a loss.

The next morning was weirder than the night before. We all had to go get our outfits for the show. I could feel tension coming from so many different directions. I knew Amanda felt like I was trying to take Deandre away from her, but little did she know, we had been messing around for a long time before that day. It was expected for her friends to feel some type of way about me as well, but I didn't give a fuck. I knew the deal. To keep my mind off of all that bullshit, I just smoked a blunt with Antjuan and kept it moving. Weed made me feel like there wasn't a problem in the world.

After we did our show later that night, everyone went their separate ways. Shatiece and her dude, whoever that was, went their way. Amanda and Deandre continued to kick it. Bianca seemed to be just a fuck thing that night, so I didn't see her around too much after the show. Everyone else was doing their own thing anyway. Antjuan and I, on the other hand, had become really close friends. Even after I was done messing with Deandre, I still tried to hook Antjuan up with a couple of my friends, because I didn't want to friend hop. Whoever

I hooked Antjuan up with didn't last long though. He and his ex-girlfriend Shanda seemed to be seeing and talking to each other more. So, I figured they were working on their relationship. He would always deny that they were though. He said that she tried to make people believe that they were still messing around, but "they weren't". I knew that was a lie, because whenever we would pick up weed from her house, I knew my eyes didn't deceive me. I saw him kiss her a time or two. She was holding on to something.

I didn't really see what he saw in Shanda until I heard her sing. To be honest though, I wouldn't have given a fuck how good the bitch vocals were. If she wasn't attractive, I couldn't fuck with it. I guess to him, features didn't really matter, and that wasn't such a bad thing. That just showed that he saw beauty beyond her physical features, and that made him more appealing to me. Shanda and I weren't friends, but we would forcefully speak when we were around another. Even though I noticed she still had a little hold on Antjuan, it wasn't enough to change the feelings that I had for him.

One day, I woke up, and had it set it my mind that I was about to just go for it. I needed something to tell my parents though for them to allow me to stay with him. So, I used the same story as last time.

"Dad, I need you to take me over Antjuan's tonight. We have a last minute rehearsal for this show that we have the day after tomorrow. Once again, all the dancers are going to be spending the night over there. I would have to stay as well." I should have been an actress, because I even convinced myself that I was telling the truth.

"Alright, I will drop you off later when I get home from work."

"Thanks Dad!"

I was shocked that my parents trusted me with them. Maybe it was because Deandre's father and my dad were really close friends, and they figured Deandre would keep me out of trouble. Little did they know, Deandre wasn't going to be anywhere in sight. The whole ride to his house, I kept daydreaming about what I wanted to do to him. Was I really going to say "Fuck Deandre!", and do what I really wanted to do? I was soon to find out.

For a very long time, we procrastinated. It was only because everyone in the house was wide awake. Once everyone went to sleep, I unleashed the freak. I figured that if I only had sex with him once, it had to be something that he would remember. For Antjuan, the sky was the limit. I couldn't really get as loose as I wanted to with him, because we were both paranoid, but even though I was paranoid, I was still determined to make him cum. So, I rode his dick like a pro until he came. After he busted his nut, he kept telling me how he didn't fuck me like he wanted to.

"Tomorrow we are going to have the house to ourselves for a while. I hope you' re ready for what I have in store." He said to me, as he kissed me on my forehead.

"You know I'm ready." I replied as I stroked his dick with my hand.

I was more than anxious to see what he had in store for me. Our first time wasn't bad at all. I liked it, but I knew he had some tricks up his sleeves.

When I woke up the next morning, no one was there, just like he said. He made me get up and go into his sister's room. We procrastinated for a little while again. After so much time passed, my pussy couldn't take it anymore. I attacked him like a cat in heat. He must have been feeling the same way, because he didn't hold back either. From the night before, I couldn't have told anyone that he liked oral sex. I figured he didn't do it the night before because he did it so well, and he didn't want me to moan too loud. I thought that Antonio gave good head, but he had nothing on Antjuan. To add to that, he fucked me better than any man had ever fucked me before. As many times as I had sex with Antonio, he never made me cum during intercourse. Antjuan was the new Sheriff in town now. Not only did he make me cum, but he made me cum numerous times. I enjoyed every moment of it. What I enjoyed the most was seeing him enjoy me. I made him cum just as much as he made me.

I knew after we finished having sex that we would never have a normal friendship again.

"Wow! June on some real shit that was the best sex I have ever had." He said, as his sweat from his forehead, neck, and chest dripped all over my body.

"I must say, that you are the best as well. I have never met a man that could make me cum during intercourse until today."

"Really? What kind of niggas were you fucking with? He said with this huge grin on his face.

"Obviously niggas that weren't like you. Don't get me wrong, I have had good sex before. I just never had a man make me cum that way. They had to give me head in order for me to cum."

"Well, I am happy to be the first to do so."

"So am I."

I no longer gave a damn about Deandre, or anyone else for that matter. Antjuan put it on me so scandalous, I didn't want anyone else. I felt like this would all eventually blow up in my face, but I was so in the moment and I didn't care, just as long as I still had him. I knew that if we continued to fuck around that I would want more than just for him to be my "fuck buddy". He was everything I wanted in a man. So, I decided to fuck with him and him only until he became my man.

Hello Love

This is for all those...who didn't think that love exist,
But then you ran into somebody that you just couldn't resist.
Butterflies in your tummy, when they kiss you on your lips...
Chills up and down your spine when they touch you on your hips...
What's this?
A figment of my imagination?
Or an infatuation?
Shit, I need an explanation!
But if I'm not mistakin', cause I rarely make mistakes,

I have finally found my mate, and I no longer have to chase.
I can finally pump my brakes and move at a slow pace...
Because the pain that I had, has finally been erased.
Since the day I saw his face, I knew I had to make him mine.
Usually I am aggressive, but that day I took my time.
But he wasn't blind...
He saw the signs...
We didn't have much have much conversation but he read
between the lines.
I must admit out of this, I got way more than what I expected.
Usually by now, I would have either been neglected or rejected
Or beyond disrespected...
Damn, that shit was hectic!
Everything that was happening to me, I didn't get it.
But it's over now, love has finally came my way,
And I'mma do whatever I can in my power to make it stay!

Chapter 5
Love Jones

I was officially addicted to the dick. I found myself thinking about it at odd times throughout the day when I should be focusing my attention on something else. It got so bad to the point that I started stealing my mother's car just to get it. One night, I went to his house and we had sex as usual. That's when I began to realize that when we had sex, it was more than just a physical thing. It was also very emotional for the both of us. On that particular night, he whispered in my ear during the act, something that I could never forget.

"When we have sex, it doesn't feel like we're fucking. It feels like we're making love."

"I agree."

As we continued on, my body began to tremble, and my heart rate began to escalate. I didn't know what was happening to me. I pulled his body closer to mine, and when I did so, I realized that his heart was beating at the same rhythm as mine. I didn't even know that was possible. I wanted to tell him that I loved him so bad, but I didn't want to feel stupid if he didn't feel the same. So, I said nothing. Right when I was about to have the best orgasm I had ever experienced since I had become sexually active, he looked me straight in my eyes and said, "You don't have to tell me that you love me June. I can feel it."

I paused because I couldn't understand how he could read me so well.

"I love you to June."

After he told me loved me, I was no longer afraid. I told him I loved him over, and over, and over again until we both came together. It was beautiful. It was like poetry in motion.

Now, curiosity made me wonder what Deandre would think, if he knew about Antjuan and I. So, I finally asked. Antjuan told me that Deandre didn't care. He would probably be happy that I was fucking with him instead. That way, I would be out of his way of fucking with anyone else. I thought that was pretty harsh, but I would rather have had it as raw as he gave it me, then to not know at all. That just let me know that what I was doing was okay. Even if Antjuan wasn't ready to be with me, he was that powerful of a man that I was willing to wait for him until he was. I didn't really know what I was getting myself into, and for the most part I thought it was going to be simple. I figured since he liked me and I liked him, we had a mutual understanding that we should fuck with each other on a more serious level and become a couple one day…hopefully one day soon.

We had a hell of a lot to adjust to at first. We had people under the impression that we were just best friends. On top of that, he was still messing around with Shanda. As time progressed, I discovered that Shanda wasn't the only ex-girlfriend that I had to worry about. There was someone that meant more to him than Shanda ever could. Her name was Natasha.

Natasha's looks didn't intimidate me at all either; it was the role she played in his life. She was Antjuan's first love. They had been with each other off and on for years. They were even still messing around after he moved on to Shanda. I honestly felt like I didn't have a chance. I thought that it was worth trying though. I figured if I showed him that I could love him better than either one of them did, I would win. So, I dedicated everyday after that trying to prove my love to him.

Natasha had a son that was just born when I discovered who she was. Thank God that it wasn't Antjuan's though. Antjuan's mom wanted to see her baby. So, that was the excuse he gave me for why she would be coming to Detroit soon. However, I couldn't really believe that she would ride on a bus as long as she did, from New York, just so his mother could see her baby. I figured if all she wanted was to see the baby, what the hell was wrong with sending a picture through the mail, email, or Black Planet even. Everybody and their mom had a Black Planet account! I knew that it was more to this story than what met the eye. I didn't even question him about it though. I didn't want to feel like I was overstepping my boundaries.

The day that Natasha arrived to Detroit, I had totally forgotten that she was even coming. I had just bought this real fly lingerie set from Fredrick's of Hollywood that I had planned on wearing for him that night. I was so pissed. When we were introduced to each other, I picked up the vibe that she wasn't feeling me. I figured it was because she thought I was fucking around with Antjuan. She was right, but she had no clues or evidence. It was just an assumption, and a good one at that. After a while, her presence made me uncomfortable. So, I just went upstairs with Antjuan's mother and his friend K.B. When I walked into the room where his mother was, I saw her prancing around with Natasha's son in her arms. I was already under the impression that Antjuan's mother didn't like me, but she made it very obvious that she didn't when she started talking about how much Natasha's son and Antjuan looked alike. To me, Antjuan and that baby didn't look shit alike. I figured she was just doing it to make me mad. When I told Antjuan what his mother was trying to make me think, he just clarified that he wasn't the baby's father, and I believed him. Lord knows, I couldn't handle it if he was.

The whole time she was in Detroit, he tried his best to make me feel comfortable, but all I could think about was if he was making love to her like he made love to me. Of course, when I asked him was he fucking her, he told me no. I personally didn't see her coming all the way to Detroit from New York and not get no dick. Whether he was fucking her or not, I wanted him to be mine. So, I was willing to put up with a little bullshit here and there, because my love for him was sincere.

At first when Antjuan and I started talking, he seemed to be a pretty decent guy. It was when he started to really like me when he started to change. At first he didn't think that it was necessary to protect my feelings, so he didn't hide anything from me. Then, when he really started liking me, that's when the lies started rolling out. He did it to protect me from getting hurt. I knew he still loved her. I just stuck around because I had faith that he would be mine.

When Natasha left, everything seemed to go back to normal. Everything was going good, until the day I introduced Antjuan to Delvon and Alanzo. I didn't know what the hell I was thinking. I honestly didn't think that they would try to pursue a friendship. They only came over because we were holding a rehearsal there, and they knew that there would be females around. It was me, Shatiece, Jassyka (Antjuan's cousin), Ebony (Antjuan's cousin), and Marilyn. We were getting ready to do a hair show. I kind of felt weird having them there because of Antonio, but Antonio had a life of his own. To my knowledge he had new woman and another baby on the way. I thought that he would have got that old ass bitch Ayanna pregnant, but he didn't. He had a new baby-mama. It was a girl that I had never even heard of before. However, he was still messing around Ayanna as well. I didn't have a clue why on earth she put up with all the shit he put her through. I guess that's the way love goes.

Usually when Antjuan and I were together, we weren't into public intimacy in front of people that knew about our "situation", but there was something in the both of us that made us not care anymore that night. We caked with no shame. Delvon and Alanzo were caked up also. They weren't really paying any attention to us anyway. They could have told Antonio everything that they saw. I damn sure didn't care. It wasn't his concern anyway. Even if it was his concern, he probably still wouldn't have cared. Besides, Antonio and I hadn't kicked it like that in months. Around the time of the hair show was about to pop off, Antonio and I started seeing each other around. Our rehearsal spot was around the corner from his house, and Alanzo and Delvon were always with us. So, he would show his face every now and then. Antjuan and Alanzo had become very good friends. That was fine with me, or at least at the time I thought it was fine.

Whenever I saw Antonio, I would catch myself admiring how fine he was, but then I would snap right back into reality when I thought about how good Antjuan made me feel. Antonio could never make me happy. One day, Antonio and I were conversing and he thought it would be a good time to start asking me personal questions. One's that he knew that would make me uncomfortable, but he asked anyway.

"So, how long have you been messing around with ol boy?"

"For a minute…Why?" I snapped.

"You don't have to get an attitude. It's just a question."

"You're right. I apologize."

"No need to apologize… But didn't you use to kick it with his best friend?"

"Yeah…shit happens."

"I see," he said as he looked at me as if he were disgusted.

"Look, why the fuck are you grilling me about what the hell I am doing and who I'm doing it with? Don't you gotta woman? Grill her!"

He laughed and said, "Baby girl, you are really on edge. That nigga got you like that? He must be dickin' you down."

"Maybe he is."

"That nigga ain't me though?" he said so confidently.

"You are right about that." I chuckled.

"So, tell me, who's better? Me or him?"

It caught me off guard that he would even ask me that. I wished it was rhetorical, but it wasn't. He was expecting me to answer, so I did. I kept it as real as possible.

"Look, don't get me wrong, you had some nice dick. However, whenever we had sex I never felt a connection like I do with him. It's more than just physical. It's an emotional and spiritual connection between us."

"What? That lil' nigga can't possibly be better than me."

"But he is!"

"You are just saying that shit because you are emotionally attached to him. Physically, that nigga ain't got shit on me."

"He is not a lil nigga for one! And it's not about how big yo dick is Antonio! He fits me perfectly...not too big....not too small...just perfect."

Antonio couldn't believe that I had said that Antjuan was better than him. He just knew that I was going to say that he was the one that made my toes curl. The truth was, no man that I had ever been with before Antjuan made me feel the way he made me feel. It was as if Antjuan was a professional. There wasn't a time that we had sex and I didn't cum. That was one of the main reasons why I had become so attached to him. He made Antonio look like nothing to me, and I loved that. No man before Antonio made me fall for them as hard as I fell Antonio. Then, Antjuan showed me that there were feelings that existed that were stronger than the one's I had for Antonio. Those feelings were called, LOVE.

Love Jones

Where do I begin?
No matter how I try to hold it in,
I have come to the conclusion that I don't want us to end.
Not to mention, my position, I am more than a friend...
I never felt the way I do, and I don't want to again!
I gotta love jones!
I can feel it in bones...
It feels like my day is incomplete if we don't talk on the phone.
Baby, pay attention! Listen to the words that I express.
I can't even rest because my heart's too busy beatin' out my chest.
You got me reminiscin' on the greatest sex that we've had...
And you have made every other man that
I have had in my past look bad.
Boy, I just want you to know that what I'm sayin is real,

43

You've got no valid reasons for you to doubt what I feel.
Every night I go to bed, I dream of how it would be...
If I had you,
And you had me...
A perfect couple I see...
Worry free with no stress.
The only thing that I would have to focus on is giving you my best.
Right now my only goal is to make you my man,
And for that I am willing to do all that I can!
I just need for you to open up yours eyes and see,
That without you,
There is no me...
Like a drawing that's incomplete.
And I believe that you believe that what I'm sayin is true,
I love you,
And I want for you to love me too...
Just give me you!

Chapter 6
The Boulevard

Stealing my mother's car became a routine. My father taught me how to drive when I was twelve years old, so it was partially his fault. At first, I would just take the car and drive around with no destination just because I knew how to drive. Then, as I got older, my agenda had become "occupied". I can't even count how many times I have taken my mother's car. However, I do remember every time I got caught. Each time I got caught, I got it worse then the time before. You would have thought I had learned my lesson.

Whenever I took the car to go see Antjuan, I knew the risks I was taking. I just didn't care. I would do anything for Antjuan. I took my mother's car damn near every night to go see him. I couldn't believe this man had me feeling like this. One night when I went to go see him, he told me some really good news about him moving into his own house on E. Grand BLVD. I was so excited because that meant that we would be able to do whatever we wanted, however we wanted to do it. We didn't have to worry about getting caught. We would have our privacy.

Once he moved into his house, it was a wrap. We were fucking like jack rabbits. I could tell that he loved the pussy, because he never neglected it. He always made sure that it was taken care of. One night when I stole my mother's car, I returned back home right before it was time for my mom to get up and get ready for work. When I had pulled up, I noticed that the garage door was closed. Before I left, I was more than sure that it was open. Right then and there, I thought my life was over. I had remembered what my mother said would happen to me if she found out that I had taken her car again. Immediately, I panicked. I wasn't prepared to face the music. So, I pulled off and returned back to Antjuan's house. When I got there, I had informed him what was going on.

"Baby, my life is over!" I said as my voice trembled.

"What's wrong? You got caught didn't you?"

"When I left the house I made sure I left the garage door up so I wouldn't make all that noise trying to open it…but when I pulled up to the house the garage door was closed."

"Are you sure you didn't close it baby?"

"I'm sure! I would never make that mistake."

"So what are you going to do?"

"I don't know what to do!"

"Well, we know that you have to take the car back."

"I can't take the car back. She's gonna kill me."

"Well baby, you know what was going to happen once you took the car. I told you to stop doing that shit a long time ago because I was scared something like this was going to happen. But you are hardheaded!"

"I did it to see you!"

"I understand that baby…but I never told you to. I am flattered that you would take such a risk though," he said, as wiped away the tears that had begun to roll down my face. "The bottom line is, you have to get that car back to her. She has to go to work, and wherever she needs to go. It's her car."

In the middle of our conversation, Antjuan received a call from my cousin Carmen.

"Hey Antjuan, this is June's cousin Carmen. Is June with you?"

"Yeah, one second." He knew better not to hand me the phone if it was one of my parents. So, I knew it had to be her, or one my girls that knew where I was.

"What up?" I said, trying to act calm.

"Girl, I talked to your mom, and she told me what you did. I didn't call to lecture you, because you already know that you were wrong as hell. Just let me come over and pick up the car. That's all she wants."

I didn't know if I could trust her to come over there without my mom, but Carmen never usually let me down. So, I said ok. When she got there, she told about this long conversation that she and my mother had.

"Yo mama is pissed! She said that she doesn't have shit to say to you. She just wants you to come and pick up yo shit from the crib."

"Are you serious? She kicked me out! I would have been satisfied with an old fashioned ass whoopin."

"Well June, how many times do you need to get your ass whooped before you learn your lesson? This is not the first time you have gotten caught stealing her car. Maybe this is the only thing she can do. You made this bed! Don't be upset because you have to sleep in it!"

I had never been kicked out before, so I was terrified. I didn't even know where to begin. I really didn't know how to approach the situation to Antjuan, because I didn't know if he felt comfortable with me staying with him until I got my shit together. There was nothing more that I could do but tell him straight up.

"Baby, we gotta problem."

"Let me guess, your mother kicked you out?"

"Yeah, do you mind if…" He cut me off right in the middle of sentence as if he knew what I was about to ask him.

"Of course you can stay here. You know I would never leave you bold like that. I love you girl." He smiled and embraced me with a hug.

"Thank you baby." I said, as a tear rolled down my cheek.

"Stop crying. Everything is going to be okay. You'll be back at home again. I promise," he said, as he wiped my tears away.

My main concern was that I didn't want him to think that now that he had his own house, that I was trying to slither my way into moving with him. I wasn't anywhere near ready to be out there like that. I was only seventeen. I guess those were the consequences of being rebellious.

Antjuan did a really good job with taking care of me. We didn't have much, but he always made it work. He would get money every now and then from Natasha. As much as I hated her doing anything for him, the truth of the matter was, she was helping us survive. She really didn't approve of me staying there, but she had no say so. Antjuan was single, and free to do whatever he pleased. I personally thought the bitch was crazy, but she was just crazy in love. She couldn't have been any crazier than I was. I use to have to listen to him argue with her every other night as if they still were together. I knew that he still had feelings for her. Why else would he waste his time arguing with her if he didn't? It was more than about money.

I tried my best to block Natasha out, and not allow her to let me miss out on who I thought was meant for me. I found myself getting a little intimidated every now and then, but intimidation wasn't enough for me to not fight for what I wanted. Whenever Antjuan would ask me to be quiet while he was on the phone with her, I would, despite how much it hurt me. I knew if she heard me, she would start bitching, and would probably tell Antjuan that she wouldn't be sending the money anymore because I was there. We had to eat, so I kept my mouth shut. Besides, Natasha was all the way in New York. A couple of phones conversations for some money weren't that bad. At least he wasn't fucking her.

On this one particular day, I had gone over to Michelle's house, and when I returned back to Antjuan's, there was a house full of people. When I walked in the house, Antjuan had seemed to be shocked that I was there.

"I thought you were staying over Michelle's for the weekend," he said, with this really weird look on his face.

"Well I changed my mind. Is there a problem?"

"Ummm…Let me talk to you for a second," he said suspiciously.

I knew right then, that whatever he was about to say wasn't going to be pleasing to my ears. He took me into the back room and hit me with something that I was far than prepared for.

48

"June, I honestly wasn't expecting you to be here tonight."

"What is the problem Antjuan…please don't bullshit me."

He grabbed my face and looked me straight in my eye and said, "June, I swear to God that I love you and I care about you a lot, but I am still not ready to be in a relationship. When you moved in, it kind of took that freedom away of me being a single man. Don't get me wrong, I love every minute we spend together. I just wasn't ready for this."

"So what are you saying? You want me to leave?"

"Just for tonight. I kind of was expecting some company later."

"Are you serious? You have got to fuckin with me? You are asking me to leave because you made plans to fuck with somebody else?"

"I never said I was going to fuck anything. I just said that I had some company coming over later. I honestly weren't expecting you to be here. You would have never saw this. I just didn't want to lie to you."

"Well, thanks for the honestly Antjuan. I'll just get my shit and leave."

As I began to walk out the door, he grabbed my arm told me that he hoped I understood. I just acted as if I did even if I didn't and fought holding my tears back until I got in the car.

I was CRUSHED. I couldn't believe the words that had just come out of his mouth. The truth was that he was a single man, and I did invade his space. I just wish that he was as ready as I was. Unfortunately he wasn't. So, I had to wait.

I continued to stay with Antjuan after that situation, but it was definitely a reality check for me. It made me realize how much of a single man he really was. That alone made me wish I was back at home. At least when I was at home, I was shielded from all the stuff he was doing outside of me. True enough, I had become his "main chick", but being his main chick wasn't enough for him to just fuck with me and only me. He was clearly not ready for a relationship despite how much he loved and cared for me. I had no choice but to respect that. I knew that Antjuan had realized how hurt I was because what he had done, but that wasn't enough for him to stop doing what he wanted to do.

One night, Shanda had been blowing his cell phone up all day because she wanted to come and spend the night with him before she went back out of town. He gave her the run around all day, but eventually gave in, and told her it was ok to come over. The whole time she was on her way, I had to prepare myself for what might go on while she was there. It was bad enough she was coming in the first place, but if they were to have sex, it would have been too much for me to bare. When she got there, she didn't seem to have any tension towards me, or at least that was the impression she gave me.

"Hey girl!" she said, as she walked through the door.

"Hey." I said dryly.

"What's wrong? You okay?"

"I'm good, just tired." I lied.

"Well, may be you should get some rest. Why are you so tired?"

As much as I wanted to say, "Cause I was fucking Antjuan all night last night." I kept my cool and said, "I wore myself out dancing."

"Oh, I know how that can be. I wish I could dance," she said, acknowledging the fact that I had talent.

"Really, I wish I could sing. Different strokes for different folks I guess."

She seemed to be really convinced that Antjuan and I were only "best friends". She even elaborated on how good of a person I was after conversing with me for a little while.

When it came down to the sleeping arrangements, I knew that I wouldn't be sleeping with him like I normally did. So, I gradually grabbed a blanket and walked out of his bedroom to go sleep on the couch. I cried the entire night, because I couldn't stop thinking about if he and she were in there having sex. The next morning, he woke me up, pulled me into Alanzo's room, and told that he needed to talk to me immediately.

"I never knew how much I loved you until now," he said, sounding so sincere.

"Really? How did you come to that conclusion?" I asked.

"The whole time I was lying in the bed with her, I couldn't stop thinking about how it made you feel. I didn't even want her there. The whole time I wished it was you. I know you probably don't believe me, but we didn't have sex. I put that on everything. I couldn't even dare to think of hurting you in such a way. What kind of man would I be if I fucked my ex-girl while you were in the room right next to me?"

I didn't believe him at first, until Alanzo had told me that Antjuan came into his room earlier that morning telling him the same thing.

After Shanda was dropped off at home, he told me about how she kept telling him that if things didn't work out between the two of them, then he should be with me. She even stated that she could tell that I loved him. I guess that was a lot coming from his ex-girlfriend who was still in love with him. He figured that I just might be "the one", if his ex agreed that he should fuck with me. After the whole Shanda incident, I begged my mother to let me come back home. I was so happy that she did, because I didn't know how much more I could take staying with Antjuan while he was single.

I should have known that the day I would have to see Natasha again was coming. This time, when she came, there was more than just tension. I hated her because she was still around, and she hated me because she thought that I was taking over. I didn't feel like I was doing anything though. I had seen where he had set up the guest room for her and her son, but that wasn't enough for me to believe that they weren't going to be fucking around. Her excuse for coming this time was because she had got kicked out and she had no where to go. The bitch had a million brothers and sisters, and she didn't have anywhere to stay? On top of that, she was still buying Antjuan shit all the time. I wasn't buying that shit she was trying to sale. She was there because that's where she wanted to be. Antjuan wasn't going to allow her to "not have somewhere to stay" and she knew that.

Natasha eventually got fed up with my presence, and demanded that he leave me alone. She started nagging him constantly to the point where they argued about us every single day. While she was arguing with him, she was making me look better and better. So, I didn't get in the middle of it. Whenever she would piss him off, he would just come to me for comfort. I did a really good job with comforting him. No matter how upset I felt inside, I didn't let that get in the way of the love I had for him.

One day, Natasha and Antjuan had got into this really huge argument about us, and he just got fed up. He told her that she had to leave. She didn't go too far though. She went to stay with his mother. It wasn't far enough, but it was better than her staying with him. As long as we were back to our everyday lifestyle it didn't matter. The only thing I needed was one chance to prove to him that I was the one.

One Chance

For a long time I didn't get it...just couldn't quite understand....
What the hell I had to do to make you want to be my man.
In my eyes I thought I did all that I possibly can,
But the closer I was, the further you ran.
You know it seems like you've been tainted from what happened in your past.
How it started out perfect, but it ended up bad.
May be that's the reason why you look so sad...
Baby let me be the cure for all the pain that you have.
That armor that you're wearing, throw that shit in the trash...
Cause I have so much to offer, but I can't get past the past.
Baby all I'm asking for is just once chance...
To be the woman of your dreams and give you true romance.
Believe me when I say that it was love at first glance,
I felt the chemistry we had after just one dance.

And the love that we made had my head so gone,
It was impossible to think that what we had was so wrong.
Please God don't let this be another sad love song,
Cause the feeling that I have it is just too strong.
Tell me, can you see,
That you and I are meant to be.
Since you stepped into my life, I've never felt so free.
Everything that you desire you can find it in me.
Don't wait to exhale...relax....just breathe.

Chapter 7
Code Redd

By the middle of the summer, I felt that there was nothing that could bring me down. I had graduated from high school, Antjuan and I became closer than ever, and to top everything off, I was back at home. I was happy. Then, one day Antjuan told me that he would be moving back to New Jersey to work with Wyclef again. Instead of having Deandre with him this time, he brought his friend/producer Chaz. The day before he left, he confessed how he truly felt about me. He elaborated about how upset he was for not being able to be the man that he wanted to be in my life. He could eventually, just not at that moment. I'd never seen a man cry over me before until then. I knew then that he sincerely loved me, and he was hurt that he had to leave me behind. He couldn't have possibly been more hurt than I was though. Antjuan informed me that while he was in New Jersey, he would have to stay with Shanda. However, he said that they wouldn't be fucking around like that. He claimed to be more than confident that he didn't want her anymore. I was no fool though. He couldn't pay me to believe that they wouldn't be having sex.

While he was away in New Jersey, me and my new found friend, Airyka, were starting to hang out a lot. I had met her through Delvon a while ago, but we had just begun to start hanging out really tough. I think we clicked so well because we had similar issues. She loved her some Delvon, and he loved him some Ciara, which was Delvon's first love. She also had to deal with a few random hoes, as well as I did. She kept fighting for him though, just like I continued to fight for

Antjuan. She gave Delvon EVERYTHING he desired, like Ayanna did Antonio, but like most men, he took her for granted.

Airyka, Alanzo, and I were all hanging out one day, and I had come up with this bright idea to do something really sweet to help prove my love to Antjuan.

"Hey yall…I think I want to get a tattoo."

"Really? That would be cool. Of what though?" Airyka asked.

"I'm not sure, but I want to be sentimental."

"Are you thinking about getting what I think you're about to get?" she asked.

"And what is that?"

"You know what the hell I'm talking about. Are you about to go get that boy's name on you?"

"I don't know." I said as if I was unsure.

"Oh you know," she said grinning. "You already know that I am not the type to judge. I gotta nigga name tattooed on me to. If he leave yo ass, just get another one over it…or you can spend mad money trying to get it removed with a laser." she laughed.

"I think I'll just go with getting another tattoo over it. I have high hopes though. I really think he's the one for me. I can't see myself being with anyone else."

"I couldn't see myself being without the nigga name who's tattooed on my leg, and he is married to some other bitch…and he got kids…but hey that's my life, not yours. Go for what you know."

I had decided to go get his nick name, "Code Redd", tattooed on my left shoulder blade. Antjuan had absolutely no idea that I was even thinking about it. So, when I had sent him the pictures, he flipped out.

"Is that over your whole back?" he asked, sounding like he was flabbergasted.

"No silly. It looks that big because of how close up I took the picture. I'll send you another one."

When I resent the picture with my whole back showing, he could see that it was only on my shoulder. It was no where near as huge as he thought it was. Never the less, he loved it.

Shanda had found out that I had got his name tattooed on me. Her reaction was far from what I had expected. That very same day when I called the house to speak to him, she answered, my tattoo was the first thing she mentioned.

"Girl, yo tat is hot?" she said sounding overly excited.

"Really? You like it?"

"Yeah, in fact I was thinking about getting his whole name across my titties."

Right then and there, I knew she was just saying that to make me upset. In my head I was laughing at her, because she was just making herself look stupid. Shanda had to know that we were messing around. I didn't know what she was waiting on. If I were her I would have been asking questions.

"Well if getting his whole name across your titties is what you want, then knock yourself out."

"You know, Antjuan is really lucky to have a friend like you. I don't think I have ever had a friend love me like that."

As much as I wanted to say, "Bitch cut the bullshit...you know we are more than friends." I just laughed it off, and kindly dismissed myself from the conversation.

Without a doubt in my mind I knew she knew about me and Antjuan, but she wanted to see me to break down and tell her that Antjuan and I were more than friends. I didn't allow her strategy to work on me though. I saw right through the fickleness.

The next day, Antjuan called and told me that Natasha had been threatening him, and how he thought it was about that time that I whoop her ass. In fact, he told me to go over to the house on the Boulevard, and wait for her to arrive. She was supposed to be coming over there to destroy a lot of Antjuan's belongings, and I wasn't even going to allow her to get close to letting that happen. I was happy that I now had the go ahead from Antjuan and the opportunity to kick her ass. The only reason why I hadn't done it yet, was because Antjuan wouldn't let me. Now that I had his permission, it was a wrap.

Shortly after I arrived at Antjuan's house, he called back and told me not to worry about it anymore because she was leaving to go back to New York that very same day. I was mad at first, because I was more than anxious to hurt her. However, the thought of her not being there anymore made me feel a hell of a lot better. I couldn't understand why she continued to stay in Detroit in the first place after he moved. She could have been living comfortably. She just wanted to chase Antjuan. I guess I couldn't blame her for that, because I loved him just as much or more than she did.

I had always assumed that Antjuan and Shanda were still messing around with each other while he was staying out there in New Jersey. Actually, it was more than an assumption; I felt it and I knew it was going on. My mind wouldn't allow me to think anything else, and I could feel the bad vibes in my belly. I hated the fact that he was there catering to her in any kind of way. I felt as if he was mine, but in reality, he wasn't. He was single and free to mingle.

I finally got some clarity about Antjuan and Shanda, about whether they were still messing around. She would answer Chaz's cell phone from time to time when I would called for Antjuan, and spark a conversation with me. Whenever I called and she answered, she always told me Antjuan was always unavailable. When I would finally speak to him, I would always ask if Shanda told him I called, and his response was always no. Then when he would question her about it, she would always say "she forgot" to tell him.

When Shanda had our first couple of conversations on the phone, they weren't that bad. Then, she switched the game up. She started to talk to me about Antjuan in ways that made my stomach turn. Although she fucked me up every time she would even mention his name, I showed her no signs that I was even bothered. I couldn't let her see me sweat because that would empower her. I knew that she was doing it deliberately so I would just crack and tell her about Antjuan and me, but I wouldn't allow myself to give her the satisfaction.

Shanda had become agitated with that stupid ass game that she kept playing by herself. So she finally built up to come at me, woman to woman.

"June, have you and Antjuan ever had sex before?"

Her questioned caught me off guard, but I didn't give her the answer she was expecting.

"Maybe you should ask him."

"No, may be I should ask you!" she snapped. "If you and him have been having sex, then you need to be a woman and tell me. You are just as guilty as he is."

I felt she was right about that. So, I told her.

"Yes, we have."

I didn't tell it all, but I told her enough. I had hoped it was enough for her to want to leave him alone.

Hear Me Out

Let me start this off by saying that I am very proud of you.
Hopefully all of your dreams and aspirations will,
without delay, come true.
When I first got the news, I know I didn't sound enthused,
but due to prior feelings this is something you must excuse.
Disregard my reaction, I was feeling kind of down.
I just don't think that I can stomach
the fact of you not being around.
You got me hooked like a drug addict ...feinin for the pipe...
Feels like my body goes through withdrawal when I'm without
you for a night.
See, I don't think that you get it...don't think you quite understand...
That it's a whole lot deeper than trying to make you my man.
It feels like I'm in a competition, hopin and wishin that I win,
But I just started runnin, so I'm so far from the end.
Between Natasha and Shanda, I don't know if I have the chance.

The only thing that I can offer you is true love and romance.
They both are financially stable, so they are able to provide.
I'm just young, lost, and gifted with a talent I can't hide.
For you, I am willing to give my all and my last...
As if you were my final and I needed you so I can pass.
When I first started this I knew exactly where to begin,
But now that I'm almost done, I just don't know how I should end.
But before I close out, here is something I must say-
Despite who you choose,
I will love you anyway!

Chapter 8
Karma
(What Goes Around, Comes Around)

I didn't think that I would be seeing Antjuan any time soon, but to my surprise, he came home in August, around Marilyn's birthday. She had this really big 18th birthday party that their mother had thrown for her at her house. Everything seemed to be going smooth, until I saw Shanda and her sister roll up. I knew right then, that there was going to be some shit. I hated that she was there. Antjuan claimed that his mother invited her. She probably did, but he could have stopped her from coming.

I found myself exchanging words with her sister while they were there. I didn't have a problem with her. For the most part, we didn't even talk about Antjuan. We talked about Antonio. She just so happened to date him as well. When we did talk about Antjuan, it was because I brought him up. I knew that she would go back to her sister and tell her everything I said if it had anything to do with Antjuan, and that was exactly what I wanted.

At least an hour after Shanda and her sister left, Antjuan received a really disturbing phone call. Whoever it was, they were feeding him information that he was not only shocked to hear, but was also very hurt. After he got off the phone, he paced around the house as if he wanted to kick someone's ass. When I saw how upset he was, I got up and went over to him to try and comfort him.

"Baby, what's wrong?" I said, grabbing his arm to turn him around so he could look at me.

"Get the hell off of me June!" he said, as he snatched his arm away.

"What the hell did I do? I said, sounding so confused.

"You tell me!" he yelled.

"I don't know what the hell you are talking about."

"You are a liar June! All that time I thought you were so innocent...but you are no different from the rest of these females out here. I must admit though...your game is tight. You had me fooled."

"Baby, I put it on everything, I don't know what the hell you're talking about. Tell me what you heard! Who did you just get off the phone with?"

"Shanda!"

"Shanda! That bitch don't know shit about me!"

"She seems to know a awful lot about you."

"How is that?"

"Through ya boy!"

"My boy who?" I said, really sounding confused.

"Delvon!"

I was lost at first. I didn't know what the hell he was talking about, but then he explained. He told me that Shanda had just ran into Delvon at a party, and somehow they got on the subject of me. She told Antjuan that Delvon told her about how I was this big hoe, and not only did I have sex with him and his brother, but a lot of other nigga's in the hood as well. She even said that he took it as far by saying that he and his brother ran bustos on me. I couldn't believe what I was hearing. What was his purpose for lying on me like that? To my knowledge, he didn't have a purpose. I just knew that he was very bitter towards me, and he felt like it was necessary to make me pay for whatever he thought that I had done to him. Now I didn't really know where all the hostility I was getting from Delvon was coming from, but my investigative nature told me that I should find out.

After I cried my eyes out and got up from my hands and knees from trying to beg Antjuan to believe me, I finally called Delvon up.

"What the hell is wrong with you? Why are fuck was you telling

61

Shanda and her sister all that bullshit about me?"

"Cause I was mad."

"Cause you were mad!" When he said that, I wanted to jump through the phone myself and smack the shit out of him. "Mad about what? What the fuck could I have possibly done to you for you to tell my man and his ex all that bullshit?"

"You told yo friends not fuck with me cause I was a hoe and some other bullshit that wasn't a good look for my reputation."

"Oh you mad cause I told my girls the real. If you wasn't trying to fuck all of them, I wouldn't have had to tell them anything. I heard you were wreckless to. I refuse to fuck over them like that! But whatever Delvon! That was some hoe ass shit. I don't think I can ever forgive you for that shit!"

He felt as if I was spreading his business, but really I was protecting my friends. I wouldn't have been a good friend if I didn't say anything to my friends at all. I mean, if it were the other way around, my friends would have looked out for me, so I returned the favor.

When I got off the phone with Delvon, I was devastated. I called his girl Ciara and attempted to tell her everything. The sad thing was, Ciara didn't believe shit I told her. She ended up telling me to leave her and her man alone. All I was trying to do was help her. I had given this girl hard core facts, she still didn't believe me. Nevertheless, she stood by her man. Maybe she acted like she didn't believe me, but she really did. She probably didn't want me to know how she really felt on the inside and I knew that shit was devastating to her, but she played it off well with her nonchalant attitude. When Ciara and I got off the phone, Delvon called me back. He tried to curse me out for telling Ciara all the things that I told her. I didn't give a shit though, because I was still upset about what he told Shanda and Antjuan. At least what I'd told Ciara was the truth.

I didn't really think that Antjuan really believed me when I told him that I hadn't done all of what he heard I did. I think he just didn't want to believe it. So, he just dropped it all together. I was glad because I was terrified of losing him anyway. Delvon had informed me in our last conversation that he and Ciara were moving to Erie, and I wouldn't have to worry about him stepping on my toes. I was a little sad that we were ending our friendship like that, but it was what it was. It was definitely better that way. I didn't need him fucking up my relationship with Antjuan anymore then he already had.

Usually when I wrote poetry, it would be about my relationship because that's what inspired me the most. However, after that Shanda and Delvon situation, it brought something totally different out of me. I finished that poem within thirty minutes of that situation. I was so heated, everything flowed smoothly. I entitled the poem, "What Goes Around, Comes Around".

What Goes Around...Comes Around

Here we go again!
Somebody, please get this girl a friend!
Every time I think it's the end, here comes that BITCH with
that shit eatin grin across her face.
Just the thought of me being erased,
Sends chills up her spine,
As sick thoughts run through her mind
on how to knock me out the frame.
She thinks I'm treading softly cause I'm new in the game.
But she didn't know I learn quickly, so now she's going insane...
She claims to be sane, but my pain brings her joy,
And she plays with my head as if I were a toy.
But I can't let that shit bring me down.
I'mma still be a woman and stand my ground, no matter how
long she's been around.
I just gotta keep my cool,
And let the fool play the fool,
Because her lies are gonna catch up...

Especially the one's she can't patch up!
But excuse me while I back up, and observe this crazy BITCH...
This chick will look you in the eye, lie, cry, and never flinch.
I'm telling you, this girl got all types of tricks up her sleeve,
While I'm screamin in my head, "BITCH PLEASE JUST LEAVE!"
You see, she feels like she's worked to hard to get what she
got, and she be damned if she's gonna let another woman take
the spot... "that she rightfully deserves".
So, she took what she heard,
Flipped that shit all around...And stomped my name to the ground...
With the help of a friend, who was once a friend of mine,
whom I got beef with in just the nick of time,
For her to do plans A, B, C, D, and E...
Just to prove to a man that he deserves better than me.
But when plans A through E fail, what is left for her to do?
Shit, rebel for the hell of it, even against you!
It's just a matter time baby before that day comes,
and when that day comes, that's the day that I've won.
She thinks that she would have better luck
If she gotta tummy tuck,
But when it comes down to features, you don't really give a fuck.
Besides, the way I back that shit up, and turn that shit around
Take that shit to the ground
And make you cum by the sound of my voice
Or even the thought of me being moist
Makes her sick to her belly...
Now I'm getting prank calls to my celly.
This BITCH got my number by being Inspector Gadget,
But when she was asked about my number,
she claimed she didn't have it.
Well whatever! Here's the lesson for today,
Whatever goes around, will indeed come back your way!

I knew that I would never call the bitch up and let her hear what I wrote about her, but something in me still wanted her to hear it. She wrote plenty of songs about me. I just wanted to return the favor.

Meanwhile, Shanda couldn't believe that Antjuan still wanted to be involved with me after all the nonsense he heard about me. So, she really started going out of her way to get his attention. When Antjuan, Chaz, and Shanda returned back to New Jersey, she started doing some off the wall shit. She would fake panic attacks, asthma attacks; pass out for no reason… or all of the above just to get his attention. I really didn't understand how the bitch thought we would fall for the asthma attacks, when she smoked like a chimney everyday. That didn't make any sense to me at all.

I remember one time in particular, she tried to act as though she were passing out, and really hurt herself by busting her head on the door knob. When Chaz and Antjuan told me about that, I couldn't help myself. Shit, I almost passed out for laughing so damn hard. It didn't compare to the other story that Antjuan told me though. One day, Antjuan started his first day at work at a restaurant called Friday's. Shanda had her mother call up to his job, to tell him that he needed to get home immediately because something was wrong with Shanda. She claimed she didn't know much, but she did know that the ambulance was on their way to the house. Antjuan thought that it was some bullshit before he left, but he went home anyway. He didn't want to take the chances of something really being wrong with her and he wasn't there. When he arrived, sure enough the paramedics were there. One of them stopped Antjuan as soon as he walked in the door, and asked to speak with him in another room. The paramedic told Antjuan that there was absolutely nothing wrong with Shanda, and that she had been faking all along. Antjuan was pissed. When the paramedic got finished talking to Antjuan, he called Shanda out and told her that her that she needed to stop doing what she was doing because she was scaring her daughter. I can't remember what her response was to that, but whatever it was, I know she was embarrassed.

While I was back at home, a friend of mine told me that they ran into Antjuan's Black Planet page. She said that when she saw it, she immediately knew that it wasn't him that was running it though. Natasha seemed to have gotten a hold to his password, and did a little sabotaging. She made it seem like he was on there confessing about how he was gay, and how he was this really fucked up person in the head, and that he wanted to seek help. She even put the address of where he was staying at in New Jersey on there. When I saw the page, I snapped. I immediately wrote her because I knew that she would respond.

"Look bitch! I don't know what the hell your motivation is, but you need to take this shit down. Anyone with common sense knows that he didn't create this page. You are making yourself look weak as hell! You need to get a life! If the nigga don't want you no more…just take it like a woman, and keep it moving!" I wrote.

She was probably waiting on me to see his page, just so I would respond. We went back fourth for a while, until one day she switched the game up on me.

"Look June, I am tired of going through all this bullshit with you. True enough, I did love Antjuan once upon a time, but he hurt me so bad that I don't think that I can ever go back. True enough, I have done some really bad things to him as well, but believe me when I say he deserved it! To be honest, I don't want shit to do with him, but Antjuan is the father of my child, and every time I look at my son, he just reminds me of him. Antjuan doesn't know that he is the father, but I do. I don't even want to tell him! I know you think that I might be wrong for withholding that kind of information from him, but I am doing what I know is best."

I didn't really know if I could believe her, but I gave her my number so we could talk about what she needed to do about her problem. When we talked, she told me that she wasn't just telling me that he was the father because she wanted to get back with him. I told her that if she was confident that Antjuan was the father, then she needs to allow him to play the father role. That's something I felt she shouldn't hold him back from. They didn't have to be together for him to be a father. True enough, I hated Natasha, but I had a heart. I would never tell Antjuan to neglect his flesh and blood. Nevertheless, it still wasn't a fact, and until it became one, I didn't allow myself to get all worked up.

Natasha and I decided that we were going to squash the beef, and do what we knew was best for Antjuan and her baby. I gave her advice on how I thought she should approach the situation. She seemed to be listening to everything that I told her to do. When we talked, she would try to slip in a few smart things to say about Antjuan, but every time she did, I would check her. I didn't care what they were going through, I still cared about him and I wasn't going to allow her to dog him out. She would ask about how he was doing from time to time, and I would tell her. I knew Antjuan wouldn't approve of me talking to her, but I did it anyway because it kept me informed of their status. Plus, I wanted to get that whole baby situation taken care of and out of the way.

Chapter 9
Sick Notes

By the time Antjuan's birthday came around in September, he and Shanda weren't on good terms at all. They argued damn near everyday because he wouldn't leave me alone. True enough, he was a single man, but I understood why she was upset. Even though I was miles away from Antjuan, I still managed to make his birthday special for him. I didn't have much, but I gave him everything I could, and he was more than grateful because of my sacrifice.

One of my brother's friends, Dewit, was a producer and CEO of a record label named, Sick Notes. He and his partner Pep were interested in working with Antjuan, and having him be a artist on the label. It just so happened that they were about to be in New York. So, I made sure that the necessary arrangements were made for them to hook up and possibly discuss business. I told Dewit that I thought it would be a great idea that he and Antjuan worked together, not only because I had faith in them, but because I wasn't too sure of what was going on with the whole Clef situation. I requested that he do his best to bring Antjuan back to Detroit, and have him be apart of his label. Sure enough, not too long after that, Antjuan came back home and started working on his album immediately.

I'm not sure if I was the one that gave Natasha Antjuan's number, but she called him one day while we were at the studio. I figured she was ready to tell him about the baby situation. After he talked to her, he told me that the baby was not all that she wanted to discuss.

"I don't know why you don't listen to me," he said, in a tone that

68

my father would use.

"What are you talking about?"

"Natasha just called and told me that she had been talking to you for the last month or so. Why the hell would you be talking to that girl, knowing damn well that I don't like that shit?"

"She wrote me on Black Planet, telling me..." he cut me off in the middle of my sentence.

"You wrote her! She said, you contacted her!" he yelled.

"I contacted her! This bitch made up a Black Planet page acting like she was you. She had you're pictures and everything up there...calling you gay...saying that you were this real fucked up person in the head, and you need help. She even had your address to where you stayed on there. When I wrote her, I was cursing her out!"

"That's not what she told me!"

"Well, she lied. We didn't even start talking on the phone until after she told me that you were the father of her child. I told her that she shouldn't withhold that from you, and she should set up a appointment for a paternity test to be sure.

She told him that she still had feelings for him, and she wanted to work things out between the two of them. She even tried to make it seem like I was calling her everyday, trying to befriend her, and that I was giving her play by play on what he was doing. She played me to the left, and I didn't like that shit at all. I saw that women will go to extreme measures to get what they wanted.

I was speechless. I couldn't believe that I allowed her to use me the way that she did. Everything she told me she wasn't trying to do, she did. I was really under the impression that she didn't want anything to do with Antjuan, but she wanted to at least inform him that he may be the father of her child. She made me look like I was a sellout. All I was trying to do was help the bitch. Antjuan told me that I had no business conversing with her in the first place, and I should have known that she wasn't sincere. Boy, was he right!

Even though he was pretty pissed about me talking to Natasha, he forgave me. I was a little worried, because I had allowed her to come back into the picture. He told me that I had nothing to worry about though. I didn't really know if I could believe him or not, but I wanted him to prove to me that what he was saying was true. He did tell me that if they did converse, it would only be because they were making arrangements to take a paternity test. I personally thought it was all a waste of time, because I knew what the results would say, but Natasha had somehow convinced him that there could be a possibility.

Since the day Antjuan arrived back in Detroit, I had been receiving private calls to my cell phone. I would get them from the time I woke up, to the time I went to sleep. I didn't really have any enemies, as far as I could remember. So, it wasn't that hard to figure out who my anonymous caller was. It was Shanda. I didn't understand her motivation, because when she called she never spoke. Shanda was 24 years old. You would think she would act her age. Whenever Antjuan questioned if it was her or not, she denied it. There was no one else it could be though. Natasha didn't have my cell phone number. Shanda knew a lot of people that knew me. Therefore, she had hands on access with a few of my peeps. So, getting my number wouldn't be hard for her. I eventually got fed up, and wanted to prove to Antjuan that I knew it was her. So, I called the telephone company, and they pulled some strings and revealed who my anonymous caller was. They told me the telephone number, the account holder, and the city and state she was calling me from. Even after I had the evidence that it was her, she still denied. She was making herself look worse by the minute.

The time had approached again for Antjuan to go back out of town. This time when he left, he wasn't going to be gone as long. He would only be gone a week. He was going to New York to shop some of his music to a couple of record labels with Sick Notes. He did go down there to take of some business. However, he managed to run into Natasha. She couldn't wait to tell me that she saw him to. She contacted me on Black Planet and told me exactly what she knew I didn't want to hear. At first, I didn't believe shit she said, until she told me that she would send me pictures that he and she had taken together. I knew then, she wasn't playing.

After I read her messages, I called Antjuan and questioned him about it.

"So you and Natasha messing around still?"

"No! Why would you ask me that?"

"Because that's what she said."

"The only reason why I saw her was because we had to take that damn paternity test!"

"Why didn't you inform me that you were going to see her at all...and what were the results?"

"Negative of course."

When he said that the results were negative that was music to my ears, but I still felt iffy about the situation. Later that night I sent Natasha a message telling her to send me the pics. She did just as I requested, and there he was cuddling up with her. He wasn't kissing her, but it was obvious that they were more than just friends. It didn't look like a paternity test was all they talked about. I felt like it was my entire fault that they had even got back in touch with each other. He was a grown ass man though, a single grown man at that. So, he was going to do what he wanted to do regardless of what I thought or anyone else. After I received the pictures, I called him back and informed him that she had just sent them to me. He didn't have to much to say. He even still tried to make me believe that it wasn't what it seemed. When we got off the phone with each other, all I could think about what he could be possibly doing with her while he was out there. The more I thought about, the more frustrated I became.

I called my girl Kay, and told her about how upset I was.

"Look girl, you need to get out the house. There is no reason why you sould be in the crib, crying over a nigga that is not even your boyfriend." Kay said.

"I know he is not my man, but I love him like he is."

"That's cool, I am sure he loves you to, but the truth of the matter is that, HE IS SINGLE!"

"You're right about that."

"You damn right, I'm right! It's time that you start acting like you are single as well. Play his game. I bet he'll become yours after he sees that he ain't the only nigga in the world."

That's not what I wanted though. All I wanted was Antjuan. I had even got "Magnum Only" tattooed right above my vagina. Magnum was his stage name, and I thought that it was cute to put that name right there.

After listening to Kay for a while, I had finally given in. I wasn't comfortable messing around with any random men that I didn't already know. So, I called Antonio over to the house. My intentions weren't to have sex with him once he got there, but just to chill. I didn't need to think about what Antjuan may have been doing, and I felt that was the only way I could get my mind off of him. Antonio and I hadn't seen or talked to each other in a long time. He was just released from jail. So, I knew we would have a lot to talk about.

While we were conversing, I noticed that Antonio's conversation wasn't enough for me to keep my mind off of Antjuan and Natasha. I had eventually allowed my emotions to get the best of me, and I fell into the devil's trap. Usually when Antonio and I had sex, I would at least be into it. I couldn't enjoy myself at all, because I felt like I was doing it for all the wrong reasons. I hated every minute of it. I thought it would make me feel better, but I got nothing out of being vindictive. It was just a waste of time, because it wasn't like I wanted Antjuan to find out. So what was really my purpose? I used Antonio as a band-aid, but band-aids are temporary, and so was he. After so long, which really wasn't long at all, I just couldn't take it anymore. So, I stopped. I explained to Antonio that I was only using him because I was upset, and to my surprise, he wasn't mad at all. He had no reason to be upset though. He was getting something out of it. After I was done, I rolled over and went to sleep, pitying myself for what I had done. My main

THE GIRLS LOVE THE BOYS IN THE BAND

concern was keeping it concealed. I wouldn't know how to react if Antjuan found out.

I was a firm believer that whatever's done in the dark, will come into the light. I was far then prepared for that to be exposed though. The next morning, a couple hours after I went home, I got a call from Antjuan.

"Hey baby!"

"What's up?" he said, sounding dry as hell.

"What's the matter?"

"Do you have something you want to tell me?" he said, acting as if he knew something.

"Ummm, not that I recall. Why?" I said, sounding befuddled.

"Are you sure?"

"I am positive."

I honestly thought that he couldn't have possibly been talking about Antonio and me. The incident had just occurred the night before. After I told him no, he began to ask me the question repeatedly, and every time I gave him the same response. Once he asked me the second time, I knew he knew. He just wanted me to tell him the truth, but I didn't have it in me to hurt him like that. He eventually got frustrated and hung up the phone, but he told me when I was ready to tell him the truth to call him back.

I knew that Antonio hadn't talked to Anjutan. So, the only person that came to my mind was Kay. I couldn't believe she would do that to me. When I called her and asked her if she had talked to Antjuan at all, she told me, no. She even swore to God on her life. I was befuddled. I had absolutely no idea who it could have been. While I was on the phone with Kay, she told me that Antjuan was clicking in on her other line. I knew exactly what he was calling for. So, I told her to just let me handle it. I would rather him hear the truth from me than anyone else, even though I knew he already knew. I didn't want to make the situation any worse than it already was.

I called Antjuan back when I finally built up the nerve to just let it all out. I was scared to death.

"Okay, here it goes…After I found that you were with Natasha, I couldn't stop thinking about you and her being intimate, and I was fed up with all the lies. I let my emotions get the best of me, and I called Anotinio to comfort me, and we ended up having sex."

He was very hurt because he was so confident that I wouldn't do that to him. He couldn't see beyond my pain, all he felt was his. I told him my reason for doing what I had done, but he felt that there was no excuse for me to disrespect myself as a woman just to get back at him. He was right. When I found out who it was that told Antjuan about Antonio and me, I was infuriated. It was Alanzo. He was mad at me, because I had told Antjuan that he tried to hit on me one night when I stayed at his house. True enough, he was drunk when it happened, but I still told Antjuan. I told Antjuan damn near everything. Antjuan was very upset with him about how he tried to play him. So, I guess Alanzo figured he would win his friendship back by telling Antjuan what happened between Antonio and me. Yes indeed, I was hurt that Alanzo would do that to me, but I couldn't even get mad at him. It was my own fault. I was responsible for my own actions. It was the consequences of my actions that I feared the most.

I Need You!

As I sit here, contemplating with my pen and my pad…
I wonder how can I put in words all these feelings I have.
But the whole Webster Dictionary can't describe how I feel…
Because it's just like a fairy tale, everything is unreal.
Your smile, touch, and kiss, how the hell can I resist it?
You are the reason for my being, the definition of my existence.
When I am around you, I am kindled with my adrenaline pumping…
Without you I am just a walking, talking, meaningless like nothing.
Okay, I am over exaggerating. Maybe I'm something,
but I would feel like I lost it all if I subtracted your lovin.

You are the justification of my sanity,
The explanation of my moralities...
Sent to me? You had to be!
But if you weren't, what do I do?
Do I just keep it cool
And act as if we never met at all...
When you made me who I am... even taught me how to brawl.
You even showed me things that I never would have saw...
Took me places that I never been that filled my heart with awe.
Is it against the law? I mean, it's gotta be a crime!
To make me feel the way I do in such a short period of time.
Bottom line... I need you here, even if it's just to keep me stable,
If your not then I'm not able
To carry on with my life...
Because you know everything I want,
and you know everything I like...
Whenever it gets too dark, you always seem to bring the light.
Look, to make the long story short, I can't let you walk away...
So, what's the word baby...please tell me that you'll stay!

Chapter 10
Madison Heights

It was hard building back the trust that I had lost with Antjuan after the Antonio incident. He was truly hurt. I didn't really understand how he could be so hurt, because he was doing what he wanted to do. I guess he couldn't handle knowing that someone could have me like he did. I belonged to him, and only him. Little did he know, my experience with Antonio was nothing like he had expected. I didn't have sex with Antonio simply because I wanted to. I did it because I was hurt. He was being used as nothing more than a band-aid.

Usually when Antjuan wrote songs for me, they were always good songs talking about and how good I made him feel. He never had a reason to write anything bad. After what happened between Antonio and me, he went to the studio the day he got back in town, and recorded the saddest song I had ever heard. It was entitled, "Ha-Ha". The words to the song hit home, because everything he said was the absolute truth about our situation. I immediately started crying when I heard the lyrics. When Antjuan saw me crying, he wiped my tears, and told there was no need to cry because he was still there with me. True enough, he was hurt, but not enough for him to walk out of my life. That's really all I cared about. As long as I had Antjuan in my life, nothing else really mattered to me.

In the winter of 2005, Antjuan moved again. He had found an apartment in Madison Heights, which was about ten minutes away from my house. This worked out great. I had just got my car, so I knew I would be over there a lot. If I wasn't there everyday, then I was there almost everyday. Antjuan had to get a job at Hanson's so he could pay his rent. He quit after a while though. He felt like the job was beneath him, and wasn't what he was suppose to be doing. He felt like he should have been putting 100 percent into his music career. He managed to do both for a while, but his pride and hunger for is dream made him quit so he could give his music career his all. Once he quit, he didn't have any income. So, he figured since he couldn't work a nine to five, he had to get his money some other way.

He eventually started calling Natasha again to get money out of her because he knew she wouldn't let him down. I hated that he depended on her, but there was really nothing else he could do. It was the easiest job he had. All he had to do was get on the phone with her, and tickle her fancy. Once he did that, every bill he ever needed was taken care of. Just like when we stayed on the Boulevard, I pretended like I wasn't there at times, because I didn't want to mess up the cash flow. I knew that he didn't want to put up with her shit, but he had no choice. I personally didn't want to have to listen to him put up with her shit, but I couldn't help him the way that she did. Antjuan was an artist. He couldn't work a job like a regular nigga. So, I understood why he chose to deal with Natasha and her bullshit.

Not too long after Antjuan moved into his apartment, I got kicked out of my house again. My mother got fed up with me never being at home. Antjuan thought that I had got kicked out on purpose, but that wasn't the case at all. I had a lot of friends that were able to come and go as they pleased. Apparently, my mother wasn't like those parents who allowed their kids to do that. She demanded that I respect her house, or get the fuck out. I never really appreciated home until she put me out. I hated relying on Antjuan to take care of me, because I knew that he relied on Natasha, and that meant I did also. The thought of me relying on her made me sick to my stomach.

Just like before, I begged for my mother to let me come back home after I had been gone for so long. My mother loved me. She was just tired of me running over her. She let me back in and warned me that if it happened again, I would be in the same position I hated being in. When I moved out of Antjuan's, it was like I was still staying there, except I didn't spend the night. I would stay until the time my curfew approached, and come back as soon as I woke up the next morning. The best part about staying with Antjuan was not that we got to have sex everyday, but it was the fact that I was able to wake up every morning and he'd be right there. Nothing felt better than waking up with his arms wrapped around my body. When I was at home, I often found myself disappointed when I woke up, because I would reach out and there would be nothing there.

One day, Deandre and Amanda came over to spend a few nights with us. I can't really remember what I told my mom. All I know was, I was allowed to stay at least two nights. I probably told her I was staying with Michelle or something. I knew she wasn't dumb though. Amanda and I had finally got the chance to catch up on what was going on in each others life. We even talked about the things that happened in the past. The good thing was we were able to laugh about it. I had obviously moved on anyway, but I didn't move too far. I went to Antjuan, but she respected our relationship because it was obvious that we both sincerely cared about each other. I no longer felt uncomfortable around Deandre, because I knew that he didn't have feelings for me anyway. We had become really good friends though.

The last night that Deandre and Amanda stayed at Antjuan's, Shanda called and told Antjuan that her and her step-father had got into this really huge argument, and he demanded that she leave the house immediately. Antjuan was at the studio when he had received her call. He called me and informed that she was trying to come to his house for the night because she claimed that she had no where else to go. Shanda was from Detroit. She had mad family and friends that stayed in the city. I am sure she could have found somewhere else to stay that night. She just wanted to stay at Antjuan's house. I saw straight through her and I wasn't feeling her drama again at all.

Nevertheless, I did feel bad for her. I knew there wasn't much

Antjuan could do at the studio, and it wasn't like he had the transportation to go and get her anyway. I was the one with the car. So, I called her up.

"Look Shanda, I know about your situation, and as much as I hate you having to stay at Antjuan's for the night, I am not going to be petty. If you need a ride, I will come and get you, but you have to tell me now cause I'm in your neighborhood."

She couldn't put her pride aside though.

"Naw, I'm good. I will get there some other way. Thanks for the offer though."

I wasn't going to beg her to let me take her. So, I just kept it moving.

Shanda called me back while I was on my way back to Antjuan's to pick my things up.

"June, I think it's about time we get some things out in the open. I am very aware that you love Antjuan. I am am also very aware that Antjuan loves you. To be honest, I think that you are a very beautiful and talented girl, the we have a conflict of a interest."

"Well, thank you for acknowledging the fact that you thought I was pretty. That was pretty big of you."

"I always said that you were pretty. We just could never see eye to eye because we are in love with the same man. I am not trying to be rude, but I'm here to tell you that I can't allow you take the place that I worked so hard for. I hope you understand."

Everything she said, I understood exactly where she was coming from, but if she wanted to go to war with me, I wasn't going to back down...especially if it had anything to do with proving my love for Antjuan.

When I got back to Antjuan's, I decided to write Shanda a letter. I expressed how I felt about her, Antjuan, and the both of them as a whole. When I finished writing the letter, I place it on the bed and proceeded to leave. As I began to walk to towards the door, someone began to knock. I knew it was Shanda because Antjuan wasn't expecting anyone else. When she walked in, I told her I left a letter on the bed for her to read, but before I could get my foot out of the door, she insisted that we talk for a minute. We conversed for about ten minutes or so. Within the ten minutes that we conversed, all she pretty much talked about was how she wasn't going anywhere, and how she was putting her foot down…whatever the hell that meant. I didn't allow her to intimidate me though. I was up for anything that she tried to bring my way.

On the way home, I started to think about what might happen once Antjuan got home…them fucking was the first thing that came to mind. When I talked to Antjuan, he told me that he didn't even want her there, and that them having sex was the last thing that I had to worry about. I prayed that he was telling me the truth. The next morning I had to pick up Antjuan and take him to the studio. As I approached his apartment, I could her him and Shanda arguing very loudly. When I opened the door, I saw Amanda lying on the living room floor listening to them argue outside of his bedroom. I couldn't handle listening to them argue, and I wasn't about to walk in and cause more confusion. So, I told Amanda not to tell Antjuan that I stopped by, but instead to tell him that I called her phone and asked her to tell him to call me. Once I got into my car, I noticed that Shanda was looking at me through Antjuan's bedroom window. So, the story I had just told Amanda to tell Antjuan went down the drain.

Antjuan called me about an hour later, and told me that she was gone. Not only was she gone from his apartment, but she was leaving the state. She was going back to New Jersey. He said that he was pretty much tired of dealing with her, but I had heard that before. I just hoped he was really telling me the truth this time.

Chapter 11
Being Challenged

I should have known that it was only a matter of time before I saw Natasha's face again. She felt that since she was paying the rent, Antjuan was obligated to letting her stay with him whenever she wanted to come to Detroit. As much as I hated to admit it, I felt she was right. There was no way in the world that I would be paying anyone's rent, but was not welcome to come to there. She knew that Antjuan and I were still involved, but she didn't care. All she really wanted was to prove to me that she was number one.

I honestly didn't understand why she thought she was number one just because she took care of him. He came first to her, and that was that. Whatever they shared in the past no longer existed, but she was still trying to work her way back in. I knew she had to notice that every time they talked, the end result would be her coming out of her pockets. That was the only time he showed her attention. So, that's probably why she kept doing it. I won't take the fact away that he still may have had some type of love for her though. After all, she was his first love. I just knew that the love that he use to have for her had vanished. I felt that if he were still in love with her, we wouldn't have made it as far as we did. At least that's what I told myself to make it through the day.

The entire time Natasha was in Detroit, they argued, just like before. Usually when he argued with her, she would make him mad enough to leave and come to me to make him feel better. It would really piss her off for her to know that when he left her he was seeing me. The thought of her knowing where he was going made me feel wonderful. She was beginning to see who really came first.

One time I came over to his house to drop off a poem that I wrote him. He came to the door, and seemed to be mad as usual. When I asked him what was wrong, he said they got into another argument, and she called herself walking out on him. He wasn't mad that she had left. He was just aggravated from all the arguing. He knew that she would be back because she left all of her belongings, and she didn't know where the hell she was going anyway. Besides, she had her son with her. As I was walking to the car, I noticed that it was raining pretty bad. All I could think about was how stupid she was for having her son out there in that bad weather. What kind of mother was she? She should have controlled her anger, instead of making her child pay for her stupid decisions.

Once I got into my car, I saw Natasha and her son, standing on the corner in the pouring rain. All I could see was her son crying his precious little eyes out. I just shook my head in disgust. I figured she was probably on her way back to the house, but she saw my car there and wanted to wait until I left. If I was her, I wouldn't have given a damn who was there. If I had a child, they wouldn't have been out there in that rain like that. Being that she thought it was cool to be stupid, I played her like she was. When I drove by her, I honked the horn and told her hello. Then, I told her that she should she take he baby back in the house. I knew that it was childish to do that, but at least it made me feel better.

When the time came for Natasha to go back to New York, she seemed to be having some transportation issues. I wanted Natasha gone so bad that I even offered her a ride myself. Of course, she denied my offer. Since she denied my offer, I told Antjuan that I would let him use my car to take her to the bus station. I just wanted her gone. I went to his house to drop him off the car, but when I went to give him the keys she answered his door because he was in the bathroom. When she opened the door and noticed it was me, she immediately slammed it in my face. The first thing that came to my mind was, "Oh, this bitch got me all fucked up."

The bitch wasn't even smart enough to lock the door behind her after she shut it, so I got in without a problem. As soon as I stepped my foot in the door, I checked her ass.

"Look, you are skating on thin ice with me. I am two seconds away from sticking my foot knee high up yo ass. I suggest you check yourself!"

Just like most scared females though, she didn't say a word. I told Antjuan that I was leaving the keys for him on the table, and once he got out of the bathroom to check that girl before I hurt her. I didn't want to hurt her in front of her child, but the bitch was pressing her luck with me. As I walked out the door, I noticed she tried to be smart by telling me bye. I just told that bitch not to talk to me, and slammed the door in her face. If I would have stayed in her face a second longer, it would have taken everything to get me off of her.

As I was getting in the car with my girl, I could hear Antjuan and Natasha arguing through the bathroom window. I walked back into the building and sat on the stairs across from his door so I could hear them more clearly. I can't recall what she said verbatim, but I heard her call me a bitch and hoe, which was all I needed to hear for me to attempt to whoop her ass. I busted through the door, and went towards her with full force ready to blow her shit out. Right before my fist could engage with her face, Antjuan's friend caught my arm, picked me up, and carried me out of the apartment. At first, I was angry that they wouldn't let me fight her, but they seemed to be more concerned about her son seeing it, than me doing it. I felt that since she disrespected me in front of him, she could get her ass beat in front of him.

Natasha no longer wanted to ride in my car after I tried to fight her. So, Antjuan gave me my keys back, and I drove myself home. He seemed to be very upset because she had no other ride to the station, and he wanted her gone as well. I was determined to get the bitch out though. So, I called my God brother, Munchie, and asked him if he could take her for me. I was surprised that she let him. For all I knew,

Antjuan probably didn't tell her that he was my God brother. He didn't want to give her any reason to decline. As she left, she told Antjuan that he didn't have to worry about her coming back. She was truly done. Just like any other time though, I had to see it to believe it.

Chapter 12
Bonnie and Clyde

When Natasha left, things were back to normal, just like it always was when she departed. Then, some he-say, she-say stuff started to float around that caused a little tension between everyone. Antjuan had a friend named, Joseph, who stayed around the corner from him. Antjuan had been hearing that Joseph was going between me, Natasha, and Shanda, giving us information about him. Everything that Joseph said, Antjuan claimed to be false though. It was more like Joseph was keeping us informed, which made him a bad friend to Antjuan. No matter how useful the information may have seemed, the shit Joseph was doing was flat out wrong. I guess the best way to describe Joseph, would to be to call him a rat, because that's exactly what he was.

At first, I didn't look at him like a rat. I actually thought he was a pretty nice guy, but he just thought that his friend was wrong for doing the shit that he was doing. I felt he was open to talk about his opinion. Then it clicked to me that he was being very disloyal, and that didn't sit well with me. One day, I was very upset with Antjuan and I had a conversation with Joseph and his sister about the things I was going through. They made me feel good at the moment, but I later found out that they told both Shanda and Natasha what was going on. When Antjuan found out that Joseph was behind all the madness, he was heated.

That wasn't the first time that Joseph had been disloyal to Antjuan. So, he wasn't really surprised. He was fed up. I honestly didn't think that it was necessary for them two to fight though. They had been friends for years, but Antjuan insisted that it happened. That same day, Antjuan came to the conclusion that he was going to fight Joseph. Shanda called him and added fuel to his fire by telling him some more stuff that Joseph had done. That was Joseph's last straw with Antjuan. When Antjuan called him and confronted him, he denied everything that he questioned him about. He even tried to shift the blame on me, Natasha, and Shanda. Even if he was telling the truth, Antjuan had his mind made up, and there was nothing that he could say to make him feel otherwise. He told Joseph to prepare himself for his ass whoopin, because he was on his way over to his house shortly. I tried by best to calm him down, but he made me choose to either be down for him or against him. I chose to be down and I stuck by him, despite how wrong I thought it was.

When we got to Joseph's apartment, Antjuan was straight to the point. He knocked on the door and told Joseph to meet him downstairs so they could fight and get it over with.

"Antjuan, if you don't leave right now, I'm going to call the police." Joseph's sister replied.

"Bitch, do you think I give a damn about the police. Call them mothefuckas! It's still not going to stop me from wanting to whoop his ass. So, just tell that nigga to come on get the shit over with."

Joseph finally told him okay, and that he would be down in a second. Antjuan just walked away and waited patiently for him to meet him out front.

I didn't follow right behind Antjuan, because I wanted to at least say a couple of words to Joseph about how he got himself into the situation that he was in. When Joseph walked out of the door, to my surprise he had a machete in his hand. My first thought was, "Who does this nigga think he is, Jason Voorhies?" I immediately stopped him, and demanded that he take his weapon back in the house. Antjuan came over there empty handed. So, I told him to man up, stop being a coward, and fight him like real men fight.

Something must have clicked in his head that I was right, because he turned around and put his weapon back in the house as I demanded. When he went back into his house, I ran downstairs and told Antjuan about his machete, but Anjtuan didn't have a scared bone in his body. He knew that Joseph would never have the balls to use it. That just made him want to fight him more. When Joseph finally came outside, I was more than convinced that he was crazy. It seemed as if he either watched too many movies, or played too many video games.

Joseph came outside with this button up shirt that she had unbuttoned, showing off the muscles that he didn't have. He even had some leather gloves on with the fingers cut out. To add to his outfit, he walked towards us in slow motion, as if he had a theme song playing in his background. Antjuan and I couldn't help but laugh hysterically as if it was some type of joke. We had never seen anyone in the history of fighting go through all the stuff he went through to prepare himself. The closer he got to us, the more I kept visualizing him doing Kong-Fu. I had never seen anyone do it in a street fight, but at the rate he was going, nothing could surprise me.

Joseph's sister chased after him with her phone attached to her ear, still claiming to be on the phone with the police. However, he clearly didn't care. So, to try get her brother out the hot seat, she started blurting out a bunch of bullshit to pull me in their drama.

"While you're trying to fight my brother, you need to be checking ya girl. She is the one that was feeding us all that information." She blurted.

"Bitch, stop lying!" I said as I balled up my fist, knowing that if she didn't stop, I would make her.

She insisted on doing so. I am not the type to allow someone to lie on me and not do anything about it. I think she took my kindness for weakness, and I was about to show her how much she underestimated my character. I hit her with one powerful blow to her face. At first, she stood there in shock that I had hit her. Then, before she could even think about hitting me back, I hit her with another one.

Joseph tried to help his sister, but before he could take two steps, Antjuan jumped in front him and dropped him down on the pavement. It was unusual to see people fighting in front of their apartment building in Madison Heights. So, it was only a matter of time before the police arrived, but that still didn't stop us from finishing up what we had started. I was beating his sister's ass so bad that I was beginning to feel sorry for her. I tried to help her off the ground, but since I was pulling her up by her hair, she was bound to fall. Down she went, and out came her ponytail. My work was done. I felt like there was no need to continue fighting, because I had already won the battle. So, I walked away and went towards Antjuan and Joseph.

Joseph's sister attempted to break them up, but there was nothing she could do. So, she tried begging Antjuan to let him go. Antjuan had Joseph in a position where he couldn't defend himself even if he tried. Once Antjuan got tired of whoopin' his ass, he got up and pushed Joseph over to where his sister stood. Usually, I would feel good after I give someone an ass whoopin', but they made me feel horrible. From the look in Antjuan's eyes, he felt kind of bad himself, but I knew he still felt that he deserved it. Once we were done, there was nothing left to do, but just leave. So, we left.

Not even ten minutes after we got back into the house, we heard a very loud knock at the door. We figured that it couldn't have been anyone but the police. When Antjuan opened the door, there were two police officers with guns pointing directly at us, demanding us to come outside the apartment with our hands on our heads. They cuffed us and began to search Antjuan's house. My mother was the supervisor for the Department of Corrections, and all of my aunts were police officers, and I remembered them all telling me that the police couldn't search your house unless they had a warrant. I knew that they were wrong, but I didn't want make the situation any worst than it already was. So, I kept my mouth shut.

"Is there a problem officer?" Antjuan asked.

"Shut up until I tell you tell you to talk," the female officer replied.

I was really concerned about why they were searching the house though. When they were finish, one of the officers came out with a knife that they had grabbed out of the kitchen. It was one of those big knives that you would see Micheal Myers have, but who didn't have one of them in their kitchen?

"What are you doing with one of these?" said the police officer.

"A kitchen knife?" Antjuan replied, as if he was being asked a stupid question. "Who doesn't have one?"

I didn't really grasp why they would ask such a stupid question. Then, the officer told us that the reason why they searched the house and questioned us about the knife was because Joseph and his sister said that we came over there threatening them with a weapon. It was the same weapon that Joseph tried to bring outside to fight Antjuan with. When we heard them say that, we flipped out. We told the officers exactly what happened, including our wrong, and told them how Joseph was the one with the machete. After they questioned us some more and discovered that we were really telling the truth, they let us go. They seemed to be more pissed off at Joseph and his sister for making a false report. They thought that they were breaking us by calling the police, but really they just made themselves look stupid as hell, and they had to face the heat instead of us. What a perfect ending.

Chapter 13
Runaway Love

Around fall 2005, Antjuan branched off to working with other people after being with Sick Notes for so long. They were moving, just not at the paste Antjuan wanted to move. He was a starving artist and he was sick and tired of being one. He had show after show, and made song after song, but couldn't seem to get signed. It wasn't like he wasn't good at what he did. He just needed to be with the right people. He began to get a little intimidated, but not enough to quit. There was nothing that could get in the way of achieving his dream.

When Antjuan was in the studio one day, he ran into this guy name Damarco who was a producer that was interested in helping him make it in the industry. Damarco told Antjuan that he had connects to the right people that could make his dreams come true. Antjuan was excited of course, but he also had his doubts. He figured what the hell though. The worst that could happen was, he could be full off shit, but he didn't want to walk away from an opportunity that could change the rest of his life. Antjuan was eventually asked to move to Atlanta so he could work with Damarco's people, and like the driven person he was, he did just that. He left and took absolutely nothing with him but two bags of clothes. He left his apartment and everything else he had in it behind.

I supported Antjuan and his decision because I wanted him to be successful as well, despite how bad it hurt me that he was gone. I was more comfortable with him going to Atlanta with Damarco too. At least I didn't have to worry about him depending on either Natasha or

Shanda to get by. That took a lot of weight off of my shoulders. The person that took care of Antjuan was the same person that took care of Damarco. His name was Papa. I didn't really know much about him, but what Antjuan told me. He said that he had managed a few popular artists, he had a lot of money, and he also wanted to manage him. I guess that was all I needed to know.

While Antjuan was in Atlanta trying to make his dreams come true, I was trying to find out how I was going to make my way down there to see him. I didn't have a job anymore, and not a dollar to my name, but I was more than determined to get there. I begged for my mother to help, but she refused. So, I figured if she wasn't going to give me the money, I could at least work for it. I did things that I normally wouldn't do like: do yard work, clean the house inside out as if I were Cinderella, or ask the people at my church was there anything that I could do to make some extra money. I had gathered up a lot of money after doing all that manual labor, but it still wasn't enough. Then one day, I was sitting in my room and I noticed that I still had this jar full of pennies. I wasn't sure how much money was in there, but I knew it would help. So, I bagged up all the pennies took them to the grocery store around my house because they had a Coin Star in there. I cashed in every penny, and I came out with over a hundred dollars. That put me in the position I needed to be in. I had more money than I needed, which was more than great.

I went to Atlanta in November. When I got there, I don't know why I was expecting it to be remotely close to being as cool as it was in Michigan. I was a little unprepared. I had brought fall clothes, but luckily it cooled down at least a day or two after I got there. Antjuan's apartment was beautiful. It was the best apartment I had ever seen him have. Papa was really looking out for him. I figured if he had my baby living like that, then he had to be in good hands.

We didn't really do much while I stayed with him, but have sex. Usually when I would talk to him on the phone, he would always be gone, but we stayed in. It wasn't bad though. I enjoyed being up under him. We did get a chance to go to Columbus with my big brother, Doobie, to go visit my other family members. I was happy that Antjuan had a chance to interact with my family, because he was usually distant. They welcomed him in with open arms though. While he was interacting, I was observing. I never brought a man around my family, or at least not one I liked. They got to meet my mom and dad of course, but never did they actually hang out. I hung out with Antjuan's family all the time. It felt good to see him finally hang with mine.

Being in Atlanta made me realize how much I wanted to be with Antjuan. I always wanted to be with him, but I was officially ready to take our relationship to the next level. I felt that the game that I had been playing for the last two years was beginning to get a little old. I was tired of the circle, but I stayed in it, because I was in love. It was obvious that I was in love with him because every decision that I made, whether it was wrong or right, my answer for doing anything was because I loved him. I had to do something about how I felt, and fast.

While I was in Atlanta, Damarco and Antjuan seemed to be having a few difficulties. I wasn't sure exactly what was going on between the two of them, but I knew whatever it was, it could effect whatever he had going down there with the people he connected him with. If I am not mistaken, Damarco was bad mouthing Antjuan, and it got back to him, and of course Antjuan was displeased. Antjuan was on his grind the whole time he was in Atlanta. So, I didn't really understand what he was doing wrong. Antjuan later helped me understand why there was so much tension though.

Damarco had been working for Papa for a while, and he was use to Papa giving a lot of attention and creative control, but when Antjuan came down there, most of his attention went towards Antjuan. I didn't think that there was anything wrong with that. Damarco was a producer, he wasn't the artist. Antjuan didn't really need his guidance. At least I didn't think so. Every since I met Antjuan, he has never needed to get direction from anyone as far as his music went. He wrote his own songs and arranged his own vocals. He was the shit and everybody knew he was too. Damarco was just a little jealous.

When it was time for me to come home, Antjuan decided to come with me. It was the holiday, and he wanted to spend it with his family. That made me very happy. The more time I had to spend with him, the better. He seemed to be iffy about whether he was coming back to Atlanta though. I didn't know what to say to help with his decision. I just supported him no matter what. When Antjuan got home, he discovered that his aunt was dying of cancer, and he decided to stay until she passed away. He wanted to spend as much time with her as God allowed him to. He was very close to his aunt.

His Aunt stayed alive longer than the doctors had expected her to. They told the family that she wouldn't last any more than a couple of weeks, but she hung in there. The longer his aunt lived, the longer he stayed home. He eventually made up in his mind that he didn't want to go back.

I can't remember who I heard it from, but I got word that Natasha had moved to Atlanta. I figured she did it because Antjuan moved down there, but little did she know that he wasn't going back, at least not to stay. He most definitely was not going back to stay with her. I was unaware if they had been talking or not, but whatever lies he fed her, I knew that they were only lies.

Everything seemed to be looking up for me. Even though I wanted Antjuan to be at home with me, I didn't press the issue because I understood that he was trying to pursue his dream. His goals had become my goals. When I first met him, I had dreams of being an actress/dancer. I still tried to pursue my dancing by dancing with him though. I believed that he would make it, and he wouldn't leave me behind. So, I stayed loyal to him, and didn't dance for any other artists. Just so I could always be available for him, I stopped going to school, because I didn't want that to interfere with my dancing. A lot of people thought I was foolish for dropping out of college, but I sincerely felt like college couldn't offer me what I wanted in my life. The entertainment business was different. It was all about connections, no education.

Chapter 14
Committed

Around the beginning of March of 2006, Antjuan went to North Carolina to link up with some people that were helping him with his music project. I can't really recall who he was dealing with. I just remember they stayed in North Carolina. Everything seemed to be normal while he was away until it was time for him to come home. The day he was suppose to arrive, he never showed up and neither did he call. The next day he called me and told me that his flight had to stop in Atlanta and somehow his flight arrangements got messed up. I didn't fully understand how, but he explained that he was with Deandre, who had recently moved down there, and he would be leaving the following day.

I tried to brush it off like it was nothing, but something seemed very fishy about that situation. I knew that Natasha had moved down there, and I had hoped that they didn't link up while he was in Atanta. The next day, he didn't come home again, but this time he didn't call the entire day, or the following day. I knew something was wrong. When I tried to contact Deandre, I didn't get an answer, so that made me very skeptical.

After a while, I just got fed up, and I did all the private investigations I had to do to get a hold of Natasha's number. I figured if he was with her, she would tell me. She would love to throw it in my face. The whole time I was preparing myself to call her, I prayed that I was about to be proven wrong. When I called, I didn't get an answer. My first instinct told me to leave a message, but I changed my mind. I wanted to talk to her myself. So, I waited for a while, and then called back. I didn't recognize the voice who answered the phone, but I knew it was her roommate, because I remembered hearing that she had one when she moved down there.

"Hi, is Natasha around?" I asked, trying to sound chipper.

"Naw, she just left?"

"Was Antjuan with her by any chance? I had to act as if I already knew that he was there.

"Yeah. They're on their way to the airport right now."

"Oh, really. When Natasha gets back tell her to call June."

"June?" she replied, as if she knew who I was.

"Yeah, June, I'm sure you've heard that name before."

"Okay, I will let her know."

"Thanks hun."

I don't think that I could describe the feeling that was going through me once I hung the phone with her. I was more than pissed. I was fed up, and I couldn't wait to give Antjuan a piece of my mind. Even though Antjuan and I were not a couple, I still felt like there were lines that he should not have crossed. He made promises that he knew that he couldn't keep, and that hurt me the most. Maybe he didn't love me like I thought he did. I didn't know how to explain his actions, but I wanted him to. I had fought for him about 2 years and we weren't together yet. True enough he said that he wasn't ready, but how long did it take for him to get ready? I was running out of patience.

Just as I expected, Natasha called me back. I was straight to the point once she got on the phone. I asked if they had been having sex, how long had he been there, and what their status was. Of course she told me everything that I didn't want to hear. Natasha had a history of fucking with my head. So, I didn't really know if everything she was telling me was the truth or not. All I knew was, he shouldn't have been there in the first place. I knew that while he was there, they didn't just watch movies and eat popcorn all day. I wasn't even going to allow him to sell me no bullshit like that.

Antjuan had finally called me while I was on the phone with her. When I got on the phone with him, I started out the conversation very calm and smooth, but once he started lying to me, I could no longer help myself. I don't even remember half of the shit I said. I just knew that whatever I said, it wasn't close to being nice. At first he tried to make himself not look as guilty as he was by denying most of what I knew, but I really didn't give him a lot of room to do that. To back out of the situation, he told me that his flight arrangements were fucked up again, and he had to stay in Atlanta another night. This time, I figured he was telling the truth about not being able to catch his flight, because if it was a lie, he would get caught.

I tried conversing with him that night, but he avoided me the entire time. He knew that he had hurt me, but he wasn't in the position to address the issue. The next day he called me, but after having him avoid me the entire day the day before, that gave me a lot of time to think about where I wanted to be. I loved Antjuan to death, but I didn't feel like he was changing. Every time I thought we were getting closer to being together, reality would slap me in the face with something new to make me upset. This time, I was more than fed up. It all ended with me telling him that I could no longer fuck with him anymore. I told him that I thought that what we shared was different and true, but maybe it was just my feelings taking control. Maybe I was so blind from being in love, that I couldn't see the big picture. He tried cutting me off to say whatever he had to say, but I didn't allow myself to hear anything that came out of his moth. After I expressed my feelings, I hung up. I just couldn't take it anymore.

Once I hung up the phone from him, I asked myself was I sure that was what wanted. I knew that I wanted to be with him, but everything you want, you are not meant to have. I had to force myself not to answer his calls when my telephone rang. He called so much, that I had to eventually take the phone off the hook for a while. I couldn't understand what the hell we had to talk about. To add to my depression, I went into my office, got on the computer, and listened to every sad love song I had. I had eventually ran across one that hit home. So, I called him, and when he answered, I let the song play without me saying a word. I could hear him on the other end saying hello, but he wasn't going to get an answer out of me. I just wanted him to hear the lyrics to the song. That was my way of talking.

I knew that he would call back once I hung up, and for each time he called back, I had a different song playing in his ear. I wanted him to feel my pain. Every single song I played described how I felt, and I wanted him to hear every last one of them. I could hear him yelling into the phone while I was playing the songs, but the fight in me just wouldn't give in. Once I noticed that he was very determined and he wasn't going to stop calling, I finally picked up the phone and told him that he had to stop before he got me in trouble. Before I could say anything else he cut me off.

"Be my girlfriend!" he yelled into the phone.

"What?" I asked, sounding shocked that he had just said that.

"Be my girlfriend! I am sorry for what I have done to you. Please don't leave me like this! I couldn't imagine life without you here." He cried.

"You know Antjuan, as much as I wanna say yes. I can't. I know that things aren't going to change." I replied, as my tears came tumbling down.

"But they are baby, I promise. I am here with her right now, and she can hear every word. I love you June. I refuse to let you walk out my life like this. I will be the man that you want me to be. Just give me the chance to show you."

I use to imagine the feeling I would have the day that Antjuan asked me to be his woman, but the feeling I had was the total opposite. However, I had never heard him sound that way before. He sounded more than sincere, but I didn't want to be wrong. After so much crying and so much begging, I gave in. I said yes, and prayed to God that he made the decision because he was ready, and not because he thought that I wasn't going to be in his life anymore. What shocked me the

97

most was that he was doing all of that in front of Natasha. I would have never expected him to do that. He never wanted to fuck up their relationship too bad, because she helped him out so much, but he was willing to give it all up, or at least that's what he told me.

I wanted to show Antjuan that it wasn't as complicated as he thought it was to be in a relationship. I wanted to make him happy, but I knew in my heart that he still wasn't ready. I didn't force Antjuan to be with me, but I felt like I did because I already knew the truth. I took my chances anyway though, like I always did, and prayed for it to work out in my favor.

Instead of Antjuan coming home like he had planned, his God brother Biz, had contacted him, and wanted him to come and visit him for a couple of days in Florida. He came and got him from Atlanta, and that was that. I really wish he would have come home after all I'd been through since he had been gone, but I wasn't too upset. Absence makes the heart grow fonder, or at least that's what I've been told.

Even though I was a little iffy about our relationship, Antjuan tried to make me feel as comfortable as possible. We talked all day, every day. All I could do was count down the days until we saw each other again. It was weird that I hadn't seen him since I had become his woman. I think I was more eager to have sex, as if it were going to be different since I had the title now. All I know was that I needed him in my presence as soon as possible.

Right when I thought he was coming home again, he called and told me that he had to go to New York and do some work with another connect that he had got through "someone" to help him with his solo project. I felt like any minute I was going to have some kind of sexual breakdown. I never knew of anyone that went through withdrawal because they didn't have sex, but I definitely felt like I would be the first to do so. All I wanted was to see my man, but every time he was suppose to come home something got in his way. Just like the understanding woman I was, I didn't bitch about it. I just kept informing him of how much I missed him.

Chapter 15
Confused

When he went to New York, I no longer had the fear in my heart that he would do anything with his ex-girlfriends. To my knowledge Natasha was still in Atlanta, and Shanda hadn't talked to him in a while. So, I figured everything would go smooth. The first night he was there, he called me to let me know he made it, but he kept it very brief because he had to go straight to work. I respected that. So, I let him go without a problem. Usually I was the first person that he would call when he first woke up, and the last person he would call before he went to sleep. However, I didn't receive a call from him the rest of that night. He continued not to call me for the next 2 days, and I was beginning to get pissed.

Antjuan had a show that was coming up that me and a few of his dancers were rehearsing for. His sister was one of them, and his long time friend, Quita, was the other. While we were rehearsing, Antjuan's sister received a call from their mother. She called to tell her that their aunt who had been sick for so long was about to past away any minute. They tried to get in touch with Antjuan to let him know what was going on, but no one could get in contact with him. Usually when no one else knew where he was, they could call me and I would tell them. They figured if anyone knew his whereabouts, it was me. However, this time, I had nothing.

I eventually called his God brother and asked him if he had talked to Antjuan since he left Florida, but he told me no. I was beginning to get extremely worried. It was very unlikely for him to not call me. So,

I knew something wasn't right. I began to cry while I was on the phone with his God brother, and I guess I made him feel bad. I wasn't trying to make him feel anything, but once I got his attention, he just let it all out.

"June, don't be mad at what I am about to tell you," he said.

"What now!" I yelled.

"Look, if you wanna get in touch with him, you can call Natasha's phone. I know you're probably wondering, *what the hell is he doing with her*... But June, he just didn't know how to tell you."

"Tell me what! There is no reason at all that he should be with her. NONE!"

"She was the one that gave him the connect in New York, and she told him the only way that he was going to be able to use her connect is if she got to come along."

I thought that I had made it perfectly clear to Antjuan that if he continued to fuck around with her, then he could just leave me the hell alone. All I could feel was rage burning inside of me. His God brother told me that it wasn't as bad as I thought it was though. She just wanted to be around, and he had to cater to it because she was helping him. Usually I would understand, but there was really nothing I could understand about that situation at all. I didn't care if they were having sex or not. He knew exactly what would go through my head if I had found out that he was with her. There was no justification.

I tried to brush off my attitude, and focus on what the true issue were, and that was we needed to contact Antjuan one way or another. So, I told his God brother to call Natasha's phone and tell Antjuan what was going on with his family. He did just that. Later that night, Antjuan called me, and I tried my best to be as calm as possible. He seemed to be upset, but he was okay to hold a conversation. I began to ask him about why he had lied to me about who he was going to New York to work with, and why didn't he inform me that Natasha had anything to do with it. He told me that he wanted to tell me, but he didn't think that I would understand. Strictly business was what he said it was, but that just seemed like a cover up to me.

I didn't break up with him, because he had me very confused. I sincerely couldn't understand why he would take such a big risk. While I was pondering, I got a call from a friend of the family, and they had informed me that his aunt had passed. Although I was very pissed off, the best thing I felt like I needed to do was stand by him, and deal with whatever problems we had later. I called Natasha's phone myself and when she answered, I told her that I wasn't calling to cause any trouble. I just wanted to speak to Antjuan because I knew that he was hurting, and I wanted to be there for him.

"Well June, Antjuan doesn't want to speak to you?" she said.

"Look Natasha, I don't have time for this. I just want to speak to my man. He is hurting. I just want to comfort him."

Natasha wasn't having that shit though. She knew how Antjuan felt about me and she couldn't stand that fact.

She called me bitches and hoes, and probably every other name she could think of, but my attitude didn't change. I stayed calm, and let her say whatever she felt like she wanted to say because all I wanted was to speak to Antjuan, and that's what I wanted her to see. She was not backing down though. She stood her ground. Once I saw that it wasn't getting me anywhere, I had finally snapped and tried to put that bitch back in her place.

"You see, I was trying to be nice, but you have officially pissed me off! The only reason why Antjuan kept you around in the first place was because you was coming outta yo pockets! Tell me what do you think he was doing with the all that money? Thanks to you, I have received gifts, my gas tank stayed full, my stomach was never empty, and anything else I needed was taken care of! Now bitch, put that shit in a pipe and smoke it!"

At first she acted like she didn't believe me, but I knew she wasn't dumb. She was trying to be hard.

I wanted her to get mad enough so she could give him the phone, but that plan didn't fall through. I eventually just said fuck it, if he calls then I will just holla at him then. The next day, I still wasn't able to talk to him. Whenever I would call, she would claim that he didn't want to speak to me. She said that she had told him a million times to call me, but he just didn't want to talk. I didn't know if what she was saying was true, but I did know that he knew that we were talking on the phone. I am not sure if he was sitting right next to hear listening to every word like she claimed he was, but I knew he knew that we had been conversing, but he still didn't call. The more time that flew past, that angrier I got. It got to the point where I couldn't keep my cool anymore, and I went off.

I went off on the both of them. I left him a couple of messages on her phone so they could both hear them. She probably didn't tell him that she was talking to me at first because I was being all nice and laid back, but once I got pissed and started going off, I bet she played every hate message. I figured if he felt like he couldn't talk to me after what he had me going through, then he could just fuck off. The more and more I told myself that I was through, the more hurt I was, and the more confused I became.

I could no longer handle the fact that he was still there. From what I heard from his mother, he was stuck and had no money to get home. For the first time, Natasha wasn't able to help him. So, I called my girl Airyka and I told her what happened.

"Girl, that's some bullshit! It seems like there is something is wrong with this picture though. I can't imagine Antjuan playing you like that deliberately. Here's what I'll do. I'll pay for that nigga to come home. Whatever problems yall have, yall can resolve them when he gets here. Until then, let's just work on getting him home." she said.

Airyka had a very big heart, and anything she felt that she could possibly do to make the situation better, she wanted to help do so. Usually I wouldn't take an offer like that, but I had to get him the hell out of New York. I knew that something was terribly wrong because of the way that things were going, and I couldn't take it any longer. I felt like I was about to have an emotional breakdown.

I picked up the money from Airyka's and dropped it off to his mom's, and she bought him a bus ticket home. He would be there in the morning, which was the same day of the funeral. To be honest I didn't think that I was ready to see him anymore. I was too hurt, but I wanted to at least come to the funeral. Antjuan's bus didn't arrive until the middle of the funeral, and it was a big fuss about who was going to get him because the funeral had already began. Eventually his mother's friend went and got him. When he arrived, the funeral was over and everyone was in the basement of the church having fellowship. I tried my best not to look in his direction, but the more you try to avoid someone, the more you can't.

He came to my table to where I was eating, and said hello to me. I gave him a very dry hello in return. He could sense my anger, so he just told me that he would stay out of my way. After he had conversed with a few family members, he asked me to come up stairs with him for a second. He had wrote this song for his aunt that he was suppose to sing during the funeral, but couldn't because he arrived too late. He still wanted to sing his song though. As we approached the casket, my heart began to race, because I knew whatever he was about to sing was about to have me crying a river. He sang the most beautiful song I had ever heard someone write for someone who pasted away, and just as I thought, the tears came tumbling down.

When he was finished, I held him in my arms while we mourned. There was no way possible I could walk around with an attitude while he was going through his tragedy. While I was comforting him, he began to talk about what happened in New York.

"Antjuan, I don't think that it's a good time to be talking about this."

"I think that it's the perfect time." He insisted.

"Well, I don't!"

"June, we are in the house of the Lord. I am not foolish enough to lie in a place like this. June, I put it on everything that only reason why I didn't tell you that Natasha was going to be there, was because I didn't think that you would understand. She was mad the entire time because I didn't give her any play. She knows that you and I are together. I swear."

"But what about when I tried calling you when your aunt died?"

"I was just going through a lot, and I knew that you weren't going to understand because of where I was. I couldn't take hearing you be that way towards me at the time."

I let him get everything he had to say out without saying a word. I tried my best to fight back my tears, but my emotions wouldn't allow me to. I didn't tell him that we were back together. I just told him that we would continue our conversation later. It was time to leave any way to go to the gravesite. So, it wasn't hard to get him to stop talking about it.

Later on that night, while we were at his mom's house, he brought the subject back up, just like I knew he would. His main concern was not whether I believed him or not, but whether I was staying or going. I couldn't say no as long as I did when I first told him I was leaving. It was much easier to do it when we were on the phone, but when we were face to face…it was another whole ball game. I tried my best not to look him in the eyes, but that didn't work at all. He just kept trying. He tried until I gave in. I told him that I was willing to just start over. I didn't really know whether he was being honest or not, I just did what my heart told me to do. After I accepted him back, he promised me that he was completely done communicating with her. I hoped so, because it was becoming very hard for me to trust him. Our trust issues were already messed up because of how we started our relationship. They increased once we did something that we knew the other person would be hurt if they found out about it.

Chapter 16
Tell 'Em What They Wanna Hear

Not to long after Antjuan and I became a couple, one of his closet friends got signed to Grand Hustle, which was T.I.'s label. He went by the name of Rashad Morgan, but we all knew him as Ray-Ray. Antjuan and Ray-Ray were beyond close. They were like brothers. When we got the news that T.I. signed him, we were ecstatic. Even though Ray-Ray had got signed before Antjuan, he never thought that he was better than him, neither did he begin to act like he was. Ray-Ray felt as if he had learned a lot from Antjuan. They had really learned a lot from each other.

In May 2006, Rashad had informed everyone that he was shooting the video for his hit single, "Tell em What they Wanna Hear", in Atlanta and he wanted everyone to come. That's when I met Connected Entertainment. They were a promotional company founded by two best friends who went by the names of Joe and Kano. Since Antjuan was riding down to Atlanta with his group his friends, I had to find another way down there. Airyka had informed me that she was riding with Joe, Kano, and a couple of others, and it should be enough room for me. We asked Joe was it cool for me to roll, and indeed he said yes. Joe was cool as a fan. I didn't know him that well, but I had always heard his name through other people. I knew that he was safe to be around.

The whole time I was in the car, Antjuan would call to make sure I was behaving. He didn't know them. So, it was natural for him to feel uncomfortable.

"Baby, I know that you are uncomfortable with me riding up here with them, but I promise that you don't have anything to worry about." I said trying to make him feel secure.

"I hope I don't have anything to worry about. I am not going to lie. I don't like the fact that you are riding in the car with a group of niggas."

"Well baby, if it makes you feel better, it's 2 other females in the car. You know Airyka is with me...I don't know who the other girl is though. I think her name is Trina."

"Naw that didn't make me feel better. It just made me think it was enough females for each man in the car." He chuckled.

"Oh no! It's not that type of party baby." I laughed. "I'm holding you down.

"You better be."

Even though he tried to laugh it off, I knew that he was extremely worried, but I made sure I kept calling him to give him security. As soon as we arrived in Atlanta, we had to rush to the video shoot. I wasn't really planning to be in the video like that because I wasn't confident in how I was looking, but when I got there, everyone that had came down there, including Antjuan, was going to be in the video. So, I changed my mind. I didn't want to be the only one left out.

A couple of months before Rashad's video shoot, T.I. had a concert at the State Theatre back in Detroit. Rashad had opened up for him, and I was one of his dancers. When I met T.I. then I thought he was cool as a fan, but the whole time he was at the Rashad's video shoot, he was acting really funny. When Rashad introduced T.I. to Antjuan, he was acting like didn't want to even shake his hand. He must have been having a bad day or something. Not to long after that, I saw a girl run up to him asking him for an autograph. He signed his name, then gave the girl back the book he had signed. She kindly asked him to put her name above the autograph, but he looked her and said, "Baby girl, I signed my name. That's all I'm doing."

"You can't just put to Janise?" she asked

"Naw you good ma," he said, then walked away.

I had never seen an artist treat a fan like that, so it kind of caught me off guard. I just shook my head in disgust and told myself to stay out of his way. I was a big T.I. fan, but after seeing what he had done, I fell back. I continued to love his music, but I didn't take to his personality.

After the video shoot was over, Antjuan made it very clear to me that I wouldn't be staying anywhere else but with him. At first we went to Rashad's apartment and got fucked up. Rashad had at least 10 females if not more staying at is house. I didn't know who would be screwing who, but I definitely knew that it would be some screwing going on. I didn't want me and Antjuan to have to stay at the room with all his boys, and we defiantly were not going to stay a Rashad's house. So, I had called my God brother Munchie, who had just moved down there. I asked him was it cool for me and Antjuan to stay with him for a couple of days. Just as I thought, he said yes.

Munchie was barely home, so we had a lot of time to ourselves. We took advantage of every minute. It was like we would watch TV for five minutes, then have sex…eat, then have sex…sleep for a couple of hours, then have sex. It was great! One of the 2 days we were there, we didn't have sex at all because I had my brother, Doobie, come and pick us up so I could spend time with my family. Doobie and him clicked pretty because of the last time they had met when Antjuan had stayed down there.

Doobie made sure that we didn't have a dull moment. When we got to our destination, which was a barbeque that one of my cousins were throwing, my family welcomed Antjuan in with open arms. My brother made him sing about a million times, but other than that, I am sure he had a great time. I fell back and observed how he acted around my family, and all I could see was him being apart of it. I felt like I was looking at my husband.

While we were in the car on the way to my sister in-law's house, I asked him how he felt about being around my family.

"I had a good time baby." He replied.

"I never brought a man around my family like that. It felt good watching you interact with them."

"Well, I am happy to be the first."

"I want you to be the only." I said, staring into is eyes so he could see my sincerity.

"I want to be the only one."

I smiled and gave him one of those intimate kisses like you would see in romance movies. If I am not mistaken, I believe we had some background music to add to the scene as well. When our lips parted, I grabbed his hand and whispered in his ear, "You and I are meant to be."

"I know." He whispered back.

When we got to my sister in-law's house, we played with my niece and nephew for a while, cuddled, and went straight to sleep. The next morning we headed back to Detroit. Antjuan wasn't about to torture himself again, so he rode back with me. About 5 hours after we left, I started to feel like I was coming down with a cold or flu. By the time we arrived home, my temperature was about 102 degrees. We stayed at Airyka's for a couple of hours until his mom arrived. Since Airyka didn't have anything for me to take at her house, he told me it would be a good idea to try to sweat it out. So he gave me a dose of the "d".

"Baby, you don't care about getting sick?" I asked.

"Not really...just relax baby and let me do all the work."

The whole time we were having sex I could feel how warm I was inside. I kept wondering how it was feeling to him. He obviously liked it because he came. Even though it felt good, it still didn't cure my flu. So, when we got to his house, he made me soup, and a cup if tea. Antjuan wasn't the type to take medication, so he just prayed over me. In a couple of hours I was feeling better. He sure knew how to make his woman feel good when she was feeling like shit.

A couple of days later I finally got a chance to holla at Airyka about what happened at the house while we were at Munchie's.

"Girl, all I have to say is EVERYBODY got some."

"Really? That's good I guess."

"Half of the girls got some by the same person though."

"What! Did they know?"

"Yeah, but they didn't care though. I think they all just patiently waited till it was their turn," she said laughing.

"Wow. That's crazy."

"I know right."

"Did any of the other niggas that were at the house get to get some ass?"

"Yeah, but it was only selected few."

"Hell naw! I am glad I wasn't there."

"It wasn't all in the open or nothing. People were trying to be low key, but you know how girls are. They talk too much."

"Oh, ok. I am still glad I wasn't there... Especially without Antjuan. He probably would have heard some bullshit about me doing something I didn't do. Lord, knows I didn't need that drama."

"I feel you. Overall, we had a good time though."

"So did we."

"We all gotta go out town like that again! Who knows, the next video shoot we go to might be Antjuan's."

"I hope so!"

"His day is coming!"

"I know. I feel like it's right around he corner. We just gotta keep praying and be patient."

Chapter 17
Strugglin'

Trust had became a very big issue for Antjuan and me. He was still lacking trust for me because of the Antonio situation. He probably thought that since he did what he did, I would try to find someone to make me feel better every time he pissed me off. I tried to make him feel secure as I possibly could though. He really had no reason to think that I was cheating on him, but his insecurities got in the way. I must admit, I didn't make it easy for him, because I was still hurt from all that I had been through with him. After I noticed that living in the past wasn't getting me anywhere, I tried a new approach. I figured that if I put my feelings to the side, forgave him, and tried to start over, maybe things wouldn't seem so bad. However, the funny thing about being in love was, when you get hurt, you're scared. It takes a while for the scares to heal, especially when their fresh.

After a little time past, things began to look up for Antjuan and me. We seemed to be happy. Just like regular couples, we had arguments here and there, but it was nothing too serious. Things seemed to be moving pretty smoothly outside of our relationship as well. He had become a new member of a band called, Jelly Bean. It didn't take much for him to stand out; after all, he was the only singer. The other three were musicians. They got a lot of attention because they were young, cute, and talented. Everyone loved them. They had shows two or three times a week. The more shows they had, the more popular they became.

I liked Jelly Bean, but I didn't think that it was his style of music.

Antjuan was more of a hardcore R&B singer. They were more like Jazz/R&B. Don't get me wrong, Jazz is the shit. It just didn't fit Antjuan's character. He made it look good when he did it though. If anyone were to see him perform with them, you would have thought that was all he knew. That's just how talented he was. He could switch his style at the drop of a dime.

While things seemed to be going very smoothly with our relationship and Jelly Bean, things at home were beginning to hit the fan again. Once again, my mother was sick and tired of me not caring about shit that didn't have to do with Antjuan and kicked me out. The funny thing was I didn't do it deliberately. I guess when you are in love, nothing else matters. However, my mother didn't give a damn about how much I was in love. She felt the world didn't revolve around him. She felt like the first couple times she kicked me out didn't teach me a lesson. So, she did it again.

Antjuan didn't have an apartment for me to stay in this time. So, I went to my cousin Carmen's house. I personally didn't want to go there, because she was staying there with her man, and I didn't want to feel like I was invading. She welcomed me with opened arms though. At first, it wasn't that bad. It was actually kind of fun. There wasn't a night that went by that Antjuan wasn't with me. I am not sure if he was there because he truly wanted to be, or if he was there because he was scared that I might have someone else there. Either way it goes, he was there. So, I was happy.

After a while, things began to go down hill. My car had eventually broke down, which enabled me to go to work. That meant my money was running out. It was only a matter of time before my cousin would get agitated with my presence if I had nothing to offer. I didn't even have anything to offer myself anymore. There was no way she and her boyfriend was going to be able to support all three of us. So, I had to do what I had to do, which was beg my mom to let me back home again. Each time I tried, it got harder and harder. However, my mother knew that I was struggling, and she couldn't stand to see me suffer like that. She just wanted me to finally learn my lesson.

Right when everything was beginning to get back to normal at home, things started to go sour with Jelly Bean. The boys had a few differences and the group eventually broke up. Antjuan wasn't too upset because of the break up because that gave him more time to focus on himself. He and his producer Chaz began to work at this studio ran by Sick Notes ex engineer, Prevell. Antjuan would get paid to write songs for various artists and Chaz made the beats. They were the perfect partners. Antjuan and Chaz still made sure they made time to work on his project as well. They just made sure they made their money first.

Antjuan's music library began to expand very large the longer he worked at that studio. He had enough songs to put out three albums if he liked. They would all be hits too. I felt that no one in the D had anything on Antjuan, vocally or lyrically. Shit, I felt that he was killin' artists that were already in the game. The industry was sleeping on Antjuan, but I knew his day would come some day.

Thanks to Antjuan's cousin Shonnie, I started working at the greatest job I have ever had in my life. Who knew that being a waitress could be so fun. She got me a job at Chene Park, which was a amphitheater right off the river front. I made almost a thousand dollars a week there. Unfortunately, I spent the money as fast as it came, so it never really felt like a lot of money. It seemed like the more money I made, the faster the money went.

I knew once August came, all my funds were going to seem like they were low. His mother had taken over that whole month. She had her birthday, bridal shower, wedding, and a lot of other random parties she had just because she wanted to book in the month of August. Not to mention Marliyn's birthday was also in August. Half of the money that I was making in the month of August was gonna go towards whatever she was throwing.

Chapter 18
Wedding Bells

I looked forward to Antjuan's mother's wedding the closer and closer the date approached. I was so excited for her. I remembered the nights when I would listen to her talk about her fiance as if he were the best thing that ever happened to her. It was almost like a fairy tale. If I am not mistaken, he was her first love, but they had got separated over the years. However, God placed him back into her life and she realized that he was the one that she was supposed to be with. I'm a sucker for love, so I cried every time I heard her talk about it.

Not too long before the wedding, I was told that Natasha was supposed to be one of Lisa's brides maids. Of course I was pissed off when I heard that, but what was I suppose to do? Natasha and Lisa had their own relationship, and if she wanted her in her wedding, that's what was going to happen. I personally thought that it was a terrible idea, because the last time Natasha and I saw each other I damn near took her head off. No, I was not about to be ignorant and start no shit at her wedding, but I knew that things were not going to go as smoothly as planned. We hated each other, and everyone knew it.

Natasha arrived in Detroit the day before the wedding. I made sure that I kept Antjuan in my sight as much as possible, and when we separated, I made sure that I always had him on the phone. Although I wanted to trust Antjuan, I still did what I felt I had to do to be sure. Antjuan seemed to very cooperative because he knew how insecure I was about her being there. He even came over later that night to reassure me that he wasn't staying with her. I loved how he catered to my feelings.

I met up with all the ladies that were in the wedding at Antjuan's mother's house the next morning. That's when I saw her. Natasha looked liked she had gained a few pounds. She was one Twinkie away from being fat. She had definitely fallen off. However, that didn't really mean anything. Antjuan's heart was too big to judge anyone on how they looked. He would have accepted her big or small if he loved her. When we saw each other, we didn't speak, but we nodded our heads to acknowledge each others presence. Before we were about to depart, Lisa pulled both of us aside, and gave us a little pep talk.

"Now June and Natasha, I don't want no shit out of neither one of yall! If absolutely ANYTHING goes down at my wedding, I am coming out of this wedding dress and whoopin both of yall ass!" Lisa said.

"Come on now Lisa, I'm not that ignorant," said Natalie

"Keep in mind that she said that she wasn't that ignorant, not ignorant at all." I said, with a slight grin.

"That right there was an ignorant statement!" she threw back me.

"How is that ignorant? I'm just pointing out the obvious!"

"Did yall not hear what the hell I just said? NO BULLSHIT!"

"You said at the wedding. We haven't made it there yet." Natasha said.

"Not here, not there, not today.... Got it?" said Lisa.

I would never try to start shit at a wedding anyway. That is tacky, but I wasn't sure if Natasha had any class. Who knew what that bitch had up her sleeve?

Before the ceremony started, I couldn't help but notice Natasha deliberately following Antjuan around like she was some kind of dog. Every five seconds, there she was. After a while, I couldn't take it anymore. So, I kindly pulled Antjuan to the side and asked him to make her to stop, because I felt like she was doing it on purpose. So, he did. About ten minutes later, there she was again. It was as if she was sitting back, thinking about all the questions she could possibly ask him so she wouldn't have to be out of his face. Right when I was about to get fed up again, we got word that the wedding was about to begin. I must say that Antjuan's mother's wedding was quite the experience. It was beautiful, yet comical. I honestly don't think that I have ever been to a wedding that had me laughing so hard. I am usually a crier. Lisa's best friend, Tyson, cracked jokes consistently through the whole wedding. He even made jokes while he was singing. I must say, he is quite the comedian. When it was time to exchanged I-do's, the jokes stopped, and that's when the tears came tumbling down. The entire time they were exchanging their vowels, I couldn't stop looking at Antjuan. I kept imagining the day we got married. I imagined it being big and beautiful, with him singing the prettiest song that he wrote from the heart. I began to get anxious as I thought about it, but I knew that day was no where near approaching.

Just like after every black wedding, it was time to get drunk, eat, and get your freak on. If I wasn't mistaken, there were more people at the reception, than it was at the wedding. That's black people for you. In the back of my mind, I knew that this wasn't going to be good. If Natasha was going to try to do anything to piss me off, I knew it would be there. Just as I thought, there the little bitch was again....following him around like she was his favorite pet. There was only so much more I could take. So, I told him once again to tell the bitch to back off. This time when he did it, he said it loud enough so I could hear him.

"Look Natasha, chill out! Go sit yo ass down somewhere!"

I knew she knew she was wrecking my nerves, which was exactly what she was trying to do.

I am not really sure how it got back to Lisa that there was some tension between Natasha and me, but she kindly pulled me to the side and asked me not to have any bullshit at her reception.

"Lisa, I swear to God, it's not me. It's her. She keeps following Antjuan around on purpose to make me mad. Antjuan keeps telling her to chill, but then five or ten minutes later…there she is again!" I explained.

"Natasha, I told you that I didn't want no drama. That applied to both the wedding and the reception."

"I'm sorry Lisa. It won't happen again," she said, trying to sound innocent.

It was as if she wanted me to whoop her ass. Lisa didn't seem to be too mad though. She just wanted to remind me to keep my cool. As I began to walk back to my seat, I got a call from my girl Airyka. I was dying to tell her what the hell was going on, so I proceeded to walk to the bathroom so I could fill her in.

"Girl, this bitch is about is pushing me!" I told Airyka. "Hold on one second, let me get away from all this noise."

I am more than certain that when I was on my way to the bathroom, Natasha was no where near it. In fact, she was by the exit. So, I didn't have to worry about her over hearing my conversation. It wasn't like I cared. I just didn't feel like dealing with her trying to get me kicked out the reception, which was what I knew she was really trying to do.

"Why the fuck is this bitch trying to get me to whoop her ass?"

"What is she doing?" asked Airyka.

"What is she not doing? She keeps following Antjuan around deliberately to piss me off! I mean, every five fuckin seconds, there she is. It's almost like she wants me to whoop her ass, or check her so Lisa can get mad and kick me out."

"Did you tell Lisa what was going on?"

"I just talked to her. Lisa knows what's up. I am not sure if she believes that it's all her, but she knows that there is some tension because somebody brought it to her attention."

While I was in the stall telling Airyka what happened, I heard a few people come in and out, but I didn't care if they heard what I said. I was free to say whatever I wanted, just as long as I wasn't starting any shit. I heard someone go into the stall next to me, but the last person I thought it was going to be was Natasha. While I was exiting the stall, I noticed these little feet running around in the stall next to me, and instantly I knew it was her son. I just laughed because I knew she only came into the bathroom in the first place to eavesdrop on my conversation.

"Airyka, you are not going to believe this shit." I chuckled.

"What?" she asked.

"Natasha was in the stall right next to me eavesdropping on our conversation."

"Are you serious!" she yelled.

"Girl yes! But ask me if I give a fuck."

As I approached the sink to wash my hands, she swung her bathroom door open as if she was pissed off. She told me that she had just heard everything I had just said, and she didn't appreciate it. I cut that bitch off right in the middle of her sentence.

"I didn't tell yo ass to come in here and be Inspector Gadget and try to see what the hell I was talking about. I don't give a fuck what you heard. I came in hear by my damn self. You weren't anywhere in sight. I am free to talk on my phone and say whatever the hell I want to!"

"I am about to tell Lisa you are in here trying to start shit with me." she said, trying to scare me.

"You know what Natasha, I don't give a fuck! Do what you gotta do. I got yo as later. Believe that!"

She was getting on my damn nerves, and I was two seconds away from forgetting where I was at, and stomping her face in the pavement.

She went and told Lisa and Antjuan that bold face lie just like I thought she would. As soon as Antjuan questioned me about what happened, I told him the real. He seemed to believe me. After all, he saw her deliberately trying to piss me off the whole night so he had no reason not to. I saw right through Natasha, but I wasn't about to feed into her shit. I had never seen anyone beg for an ass whoopin' like she did. As much as I wanted to grant her wish, I couldn't allow myself to do that. I refuse to give her the satisfaction.

While I was sitting at the table eating with my girl Frances, I noticed that Antjuan and a couple of his friends had stepped outside. So, I looked around to see if Natasha was anywhere to be found as well, and sure enough she was outside. That was my last straw. I approached Antjuan again, and told him to get that bitch before I did, because I was getting tired of her disrespecting me. I made sure she heard me clear as day. After I said that, I noticed that she had said something under hear breath.

"Bitch, speak up! I advise you to fall back or we are going to have some serious problems."

She didn't say a word. She just kept it moving.

"I don't know why you are playin yourself like that. He moved on, and I think that it's time that you do the same.

She stopped in her tracks, turned around and looked me straight in the eye.

"Moved on? To who? You?" she asked.

"Bitch, why are you actin brand new? You know me and Antjuan are together.

"Oh really? If yall are together, than why was he fucking me last night?" she threw at me.

I must say, she caught me off guard with that one. I didn't even give a fuck about her anymore, I went straight to Antjuan.

"So, you fucked Natasha last night?"

"June, don't be naive. I was with you last night and you know that."

"You weren't with me the entire night."

"When I wasn't with you, I was with the groomsmen, and you knew that. Baby, she is lying. I swear to God."

When he called her a liar in her face, and put all the facts out there of his whereabouts, I knew she was embarrassed. After Antjuan did that, she stormed off and stayed to herself the rest of night. In fact, Antjuan told her that she was no longer allowed to come back into the reception because she didn't know how to act. So, she took her son and sat in the car until the reception was over. My day was made. I always waited for the day that I came before her, and my day had finally come. I knew then that I won Antjuan's heart. When the reception was over, Antjuan and I left together. I couldn't help but laugh because I saw Natasha staring at us the entire time. Antjuan wasn't holding back at all. He made sure she knew we were together, since she acted like she was so unsure.

Chapter 19
Getting Twisted

When the summer of 2006 rolled around, I felt that it was time for Antjuan to stop trying to do everything on his own. I knew that Antjuan needed a manager bad and fast. So, I took it upon myself to try and find him one. I really didn't know where to begin, but I figured I would start with the people that I knew that was in the entertainment industry. I asked a few party promoters that I knew that were also managers of other artist, but they all seem to be iffy about doing it. It wasn't my style to beg. So, I just kept it moving. I even asked a couple of people that worked at the radio station, and dj's if they knew someone that would be interested...but still, they seemed kind of iffy. I didn't get it. It wasn't like they didn't know who he was. They all thought he was the shit, but they also gave me some weird ass reason of why they couldn't.

I found out that the reason why people were acting so iffy about Antjuan, was because Damarco had been spitting venom on his name. Detroit isn't that big, and the entertainment industry in the D isn't that big either. So, whatever he was saying got around. Damarco was telling people that Antjuan had a lot of personal issues and he was a very difficult person to work with. He tried to make it clear that he was a waste of talent basically. When Antjuan found out that he was saying all of these things, he was highly pissed. He knew why he was doing it though. Damarco figured, if he wasn't going work with him, he wasn't going to work with anybody, and he tried his best to sabotage him.

One day, Airyka and I decided to throw a little get together at her house. It wasn't for any special occasion. It was just because, and only selected few were invited. Two people that were invited were Ian and Twist of Twisted Entertainment. I didn't really know much about them. I had just seen them around the way a couple of times, but I knew they had something to do with the entertainment industry. I didn't ask them right off the back if they wanted to work with Antjuan, or if they knew someone that did. I just popped in one of Antjuan's cd's and observed how they responded it to it. They were all in.

"June, why you never told me about ya boy?" said Twist.

"I did. You obviously wasn't paying attention."

"I must've been buzzin or something, cause this nigga is hot!"

"I just didn't have his music on me at the time, that's all."

They had no idea that Antjuan was that good. Immediately they wanted to work with him.

"Yo, I am looking for management right now if you didn't know," said Antjuan.

"Shit, I'll manage yo ass! You got talent my dude. I'm surprised you don't have one already," said Ian, showing how he excited he was to be working with such a talented artist.

"Well, you know what hey say...everything happens in season," said Antjuan, trying to be humble.

"Your right about that!" said Twist.

They exchanged numbers after conversing for about 2 hours, and Ian and Twist told him that they were about to show him how serious they really were about wanting to work for him.

Every day after the party at Airyka's, Ian and Twist dedicated damn near all of their time and money towards Antjuan. They took good care of him. He never needed for anything. The best part was, he was doing shows again. That meant I was dancing again. Antjuan didn't have the same dancers he usually had though. It was me, Chiquita, Monica, Jameka, Akinyale', and this girl that I didn't care too much for name, Denisha. Now the reason why I didn't like Denisha was for a couple of reasons. She was sneaky as fuck. She had tried to get on my girl Airyka's dude, and she knew that they were kicking it because they were always with each other. Even if he tried to get on her, it was disrespectful to even give him the time of day because she knew the deal. I had also heard a lot of random things about her. However, I knew she liked Antjuan, and that was the icing on the cake for me. I wasn't crazy. A woman knows when another woman is feeling her man, and it was written all over her face.

One day, my God-mother called me and asked me if I could come over and watch her foster kids for about a week. I loved my God-mother. So, I didn't have a problem with it at all. She paid me and she allowed me to use my God-sister Jackie's car when I needed it. So, that was a plus. Antjuan was there with me just about every day. On one particular day, Antjuan got caught slippin. He went to sleep, and his cell phone was calling my name to go through it. I didn't like going through Antjuan's phone because I wanted to respect his privacy, but I had been having that feeling that Antjuan wasn't being as faithful as he claimed to be. So, while he was sleeping, I took his phone, went to a different room, and began my Inspector Gadget mission.

Antjuan had deleted all of his outgoing calls, texts, and missed calls. I knew then that he had something to hide. If he wasn't talking to other women then there was no reason for him to delete his call log. Suddenly, it dawned on me that I didn't check Antjuan's incoming calls. I figured if he deleted everything else then I shouldn't find anything. However, I thought I should try any way. To my surprise he didn't delete his incoming calls. I saw a few numbers in there that didn't have a name to them, and I figured that they were females, because he wasn't dumb enough to store the female's numbers in his phone. I called all the unknown numbers blocked to see if they were females. Most of them were people that I knew, but not females. It wasn't until I got to the end of my list when I ran into a girl or two. I was highly pissed off. Antjuan had told me that he hadn't talk to absolutely no other females. I should have known better though.

I couldn't control how mad I was. So, I woke Antjuan up and told him that it was time for me to take him home. He was so sleepy, he didn't question why. He just got up and did as I asked. The entire time we were in the car, I said absolutely nothing to him. When we pulled up in front of his house, I waited until he got out the car, and that's when I started asking questions.

"So, have you been talking to any females lately?" I asked, knowing that he was about to lie to me.

"No...why would you ask me that?" he said, with this confused look on his face.

"Because I wanted to see if you were going to be honest... But you're just a fuckin liar!" I yelled.

"What the fuck are you talking about?" he yelled back at me.

"May be next time you erase your call log, make sure you erase your ENTIRE call log. May be you won't get caught...but I got the numbers to ya little female friends that you have been talking to. I will call them later to see what's really poppin!" I said, trying to scare him.

I rolled up the window, and proceeded to reverse out the driveway. I heard him saying something back to me, but I figured it was some bullshit. So, I just rolled up the window and drove off.

While I was at the doctor's office with one of the foster kids, I called those females' numbers back. One of the girls was someone I knew. She was actually a friend of his sister's and she was calling his phone looking for her. It wasn't until I called the second number where my world got turned upside down. Her name was Ryana. She was very cooperative. When I asked her questions, she gave me straight up answers.

"So, have you been seeing Antjuan intimately?" I asked, hoping that the answer would be no even though I knew the truth.

"Yes I have," she said calmly.

"Really? How long has been this been going on?"

"For a couple of months."

"A couple of months? Are you serious!"

"Yep!" she said so confidently.

"Did you know he had a girlfriend?" I asked.

"He told me that you two had broke up, but I knew that you two were still involved because I would see you call his phone all the time."

She began to tell me about a lot of times that they had spent together, all the people that she met through him, and all the places she had been, which made me sick to my stomach. I knew that she couldn't have possibly spent as much time as she claimed to with him though. She obviously didn't know our status and how much he was around me. A lot of what she said was fabricated, because Antjuan spent damn near everyday, all day with me. He may have fucked with her from time to time, but it wasn't anywhere near how she described it to be.

When I approached Antjuan and told him that I knew that he had been cheating, he tried to deny it at first, but when I started telling him stories that he couldn't deny, he knew then it was a wrap. He was caught and there was no backing out. He started apologizing to me and telling me that he never meant to hurt me like that, and it wasn't as deep as I thought it was, but everything he was saying to me was going through one ear and out of the other. All I could see was him making love to her like he did me and that was the worst image I could ever have in my head. I told him that I didn't want anything to do with him, and once again I began to ignore every call and text to my phone. I knew that I still loved him, and I wasn't really sure if I was really going to walk away. I was just very upset and disappointed with him.

I really didn't have it in me to talk to him, so I asked my God sister Jackie to talk to him instead. He poured his heart out to her, and Jackie told me everything he said, but I still didn't give in. Once Jackie got off the phone with her, she tried her best to console me because she knew that I was in a lot of pain.

"You know June, I know that you are hurting...but can you be real with me? Are you going to stop fucking with him?"

"I feel like I have no choice but to stop messing with him. I am tired of being hurt."

"No one likes to be hurt. I know that he fucked up, and it wasn't the first time. It probably won't be the last. He is young, and he is a man on top of everything else. You know how weak men are. He will eventually grow out of doing that dumb shit he is doing. That man loves you."

"I never doubted that he loved me Jackie. I just don't know how much more I can deal with."

"Well, I know how much you love him…and I can tell you right now that this is not the end. You still have some more fight in you. The love that you have for Antjuan, is something amazing. I can't even describe it."

Even though Jackie was younger than me, I still listened to her because I knew she was right. The next day, Antjuan had to go out of town. So, he tried his hardest to make sure that he got in touch with me before he left. I finally answered his calls and allowed him to come and talk to me. No matter how mad I was at him, I just couldn't let him go. He begged for my forgiveness and asked me not to try to get back at him back for what he had done to me. I followed my heart and I forgave him, and accepted him as my boyfriend again, but the thought of him cheating on me never vanished. I think I should have given myself some time to heal, because I was far from over it.

Not too long after the Ryana situation, I got in touch with a dude I use to talk to back in high school name, Chris. I couldn't shake the fact that I was still hurt over what Antjuan had done to me. I think I was more pissed off at the fact that they had been fucking with each other for over a month. That's what ate me up the most. He didn't just hit it and quit. He built somewhat of a relationship with the bitch. So once again, to make myself feel better, I chose to be vindictive. I knew that this time, I didn't have to worry about him finding out. Chris knew that I was using him, but he didn't care. What man would? I really didn't understand why I chose to go that route again because every time I did, I felt like shit the entire time I did, and even worse afterwards. After I had sex with Chris for the third time, I couldn't take it anymore. It wasn't like we had an emotional connection. I was just doing it to get back at Antjuan. I figured that if I was going to disrespect myself and my relationship to make myself feel better about something, then I don't need to be in it. However, I knew that Antjuan had my heart, and I didn't want to leave. I never told Antjuan what I'd done, and I knew that he would never find out. I just wanted to bury it, and act as if it never happened. I felt guilty everyday, but I didn't have the courage to break his heart. So, I promised myself to just take it to the grave. I knew that there was no possible way that I could ever be vindictive again, no matter what he did. I was either going to leave him, or forgive him or stay with him and pray that things get better.

Chapter 20
Making the Band

In the summer of 2006 Antjuan's life began to alter. Antjuan was grateful for all that Ian and Twist had done for him, but he felt it was time that he stopped doing unpaid shows. Antjuan was ready to make that paper. He felt that he had made a name in Detroit, and people shouldn't mind showing that love to support, and I agreed. One day, Antjuan went with a friend to his movie rehearsal/audition. While he was there, he decided to tryout and without a doubt he got the part. Antjuan was very excited about being in a movie. This was a very big step for him. Whether it was big or local, it was good exposure and he was getting paid.

The name of the movie was called, *Diary of a Champion*. I don't remember fully what it was about, but I know it had something to do with the Olympics, and it required for him to get up every morning and run the track as if he was on the track team. In fact, it was about a track star that won the Olympics, with a couple of twist and turns to make it a good movie of course.

Then one of the casting members name, Rodney, who had become really good friends with Antjuan, told him that Making the Band was having auditions in Detroit which took place in February, and that he should go audition. Antjuan said that he was already thinking about going after seeing the advertisement on TV. I wanted Antjuan to be a solo artist really bad. However, you have to crawl before you walk, and I thought it was a very good idea.

"I won two VIP bracelets from the radio station for the Making the

127

Band 4 auditions. With this bracelet, you don't have to wait in line at all. You can just go straight to the front of the line and they will let you in. On top of that, you choose when you want to audition once you get in," said Rodney.

"Straight up! You plan on auditioning!" Antjuan asked, acting overly excited.

"Come on man! Have you ever known me to be a singer. Their yours. I couldn't think of anyone else to give them to. You deserve them. Besides, I already know that you're gonna win."

"Thanks man, I really appreciate it!"

I knew that once Antjuan received that bracelet, that it was going to be a wrap.

The day of the audition had to be one of the coldest days in Detroit. Antjuan was lucky that he didn't have to stand outside in that long ass line that wrapped half way around the corner. For moral support, he had me and his boy, Mike, come along with him. Mike was actually nice enough to drive us to the audition. He believed that Antjuan was going to make the audition without a doubt, and he made sure that he made it there. Antjuan had an extra wristband. So, he gave it to his boy John Brown, which was one of his former group members. I knew that both of them would make it. They both had some very beautiful voices.

While they auditioned, Mike and I waited patiently for the results. When Antjuan came out, he tried to fake like he didn't make it, but I knew he was full of shit. There was no way they could deny him. He could sing, dance, and he had the look. What more could they ask for? He told us that he was the first one to audition, and the judges loved him, and so did everyone else that was auditioning. I knew then that Antjuan's life was about to change. His boy John Brown made it as well, but the audition they made wasn't the last audition they had to do. They had to audition again the next day, and it required them to dance. Dancing was nothing to Antjuan. So, I didn't worry about him not making that audition, but John wasn't much of a dancer and that's when he got intimidated. The next day at the second audition, Antjuan made it, just as I predicted. However, his friend was sadly eliminated. Antjuan didn't have long before it was time for him to go to New York, to start taping for the show. I was so excited for him. I just kept imagining the finale, where Diddy was going to call his name and tell him that he made the band. I just knew it was going to happen. We spent as much time as we possibly could before he left. I knew that this was going to be the longest period we would be away from each other, and I also knew that I was a very determined woman, and I was going to make my way to New York eventually. The day Antjuan left, I was the saddest woman in Detroit, but I was also the proudest at the same time. It was time for Antjuan to shine, and I wasn't going to hold him back from it.

Antjuan made sure he called me everyday while he was there. When he first arrived, they all had to stay in a hotel, until they cut down all 58 men that made it to New York down to 20. The day before Antjuan was about to move into the house, we had a discussion about a party that I had been invited to. I knew Antjuan didn't like me hanging with the party crowd. However, it was my girl's, Xplicit Lyric's, mixtape release party and I wanted to support her. I told him that I wasn't going, but the next day I changed my mind.

I hadn't talked to Antjuan the entire next day. I knew he was supposed to move into the house, but I had no way to get in contact him. I wanted to at least inform him that I had changed my mind. While I was at the party, Antjuan's assistant manager, Twist, came to me and told me that Antjuan was trying to get in touch with me, but when I tried to call back the line was busy. I knew that he was going to be pissed off when I spoke to him. When I got home, I called him and that's when he asked me about the party and who I went with.

"So where were you June?" he asked, but I knew he already knew the answer to the question.

"I went to XL album release party."

"I thought you said you wasn't going."

"Well, I changed my mind. Is there a problem?" I replied, knowing that there was a about to be a major one.

"You changed your mind?! I have been trying to get in contact with you all day. I have been blowin' up yo' shit, and everybody else shit! You knew that I was going to be calling you, I just don't understand why the fuck you wouldn't be waiting on my phone call!" He yelled into the phone.

"There is nothing wrong about me going support my girl! At first I wasn't going to go, but then I changed my mind...and besides, I tried calling you to let you know what was up, but I couldn't get in contact with you!" I yelled back.

"So who did you go to the party with?"

"Michelle." I lied.

"Why the fuck are you lying? You didn't go with no fuckin Michelle!"

I really went with his cousin, who was a female, but I didn't want to get her in trouble for taking me. I felt bad for lying to him, but I still felt like he was blowing that whole situation out of proportion. I just went to a party to support my girl. The club was packed full of people he knew. So, me doing something I had no business doing was out of the question. Besides, I wasn't on that shit anyway. We ended the conversation very bitterly. He hung up in my face after I called him a "drama king", and when I tried to call back, he didn't answer the phone for the remainder of the night. He still acted bitter towards me for a couple of days, but after a while we made up and everything was cool after that.

Just when I thought that everything was good, I received a call from Shanda. She was the last person I was expecting to hear from, and the last person I wanted to hear from. She told me that she had been talking to Antjuan while he was in New York, and that she saw him a couple of times. The first thing that ran through my mind was, "Is this nigga really playing me like that on national television?" I was pissed. At first I didn't believe her, until she called him on three-way.

"Hello, can I speak to Robert?" she asked.

"This is me."

"Hey, I need to talk to you, but I don't want to talk over these phones. Can you meet me somewhere?"

"Yeah, but it will have to be later." He replied, not knowing what he was getting himself into.

After she hung up with him, I immediately called him back. "So why haven't you called me all day?" I asked, waiting to see what bullshit he was about to feed me.

"Baby, we just got in the house not too long ago, I haven't talked to anyone."

"You haven't talked to NO BODY!"

"No June! What the fuck is the problem?"

After he said that, I snapped. I really didn't know to what extent Shanda and Antjuan had communicated, but I was fed up with the bullshit. Without even thinking, I broke up with him. I didn't care about our phone conversation being recorded or anything. I was too pissed to even think about it.

When I had finally calmed down, I called him back, but unfortunately he was in the middle of practicing. He talked to me very briefly because he had to get back to work. After a couple of hours past, I noticed that he still hadn't called. So, I called him back again. He was still rehearsing is what he told me. I didn't really know if he was telling me the truth. I just thought that he was acting upset because I had dumped him. When we finally spoke again, he explained to me that seeing Shanda wasn't really what it seemed. She knew about the elimination they had at BB Kings, and she came, and that's when he saw her. He said that he was just being nice by giving her the number to the house. I didn't really believe him, but when I talked to Shanda she told me that they hadn't been talking on the level I assumed they had been. She really pissed me off because I didn't believe her anymore than I did him. I didn't understand her purpose for calling me and making it seem like it was something more than it was if it wasn't.

I made the decision to just drop the situation. If he was telling me the truth or not, I would never really know. I just wanted to move on. When I was ready to get back with him, he wasn't. He seemed to be very pissed off about me dumping on him on national television. What he failed to realize was, I was upset that he would talk to his ex-girl on national TV, like it was nothing worth me being upset or embarrassed about. I gave him his time to get over what I had done. Then, one day I wrote him a poem. The day after I read it to him, he got news that he was about to come home, and it was the day before my birthday. That day he asked me to be his girlfriend again.

Can't Let Go

It's sad....
I think I really got it bad,
cause I can't seem to keep my fingers of of this dialing pad.
It Seems like just yesterday, I tried to put it in the bag,
throw it all away, and forget about the love that we had...
but come on, let's be logical.
You know that it's impossible.
It's all psychological...
and even more illogical.
Can you hear me baby, I am calling out your name.
Since I put you out my life everything ain't been the same.
It's funny how I still keep you pictures in a frame...
and claim your last name like ain't shit changed.
Now, Is that lame?
or a God damn shame,
that your addictive like a drug, and fiend I became.
I can feel u in my veins....
playing with brain...
driving me insane...
but baby I can't complain...
Cause the feeling that I feel, is also the best I've ever felt.

It's like I can't get enough, but your hazardess to my health.
So, what's a girl to do when she says "We're through!"
but stuck like glue, to a nigga like you.
I don't get it! Can you help me understand?
Letting go might be what's best, but I don't
think that I can.

Chapter 21
The Finale

The time had come for Diddy to finally make the band, or at least I thought it was time. I had gathered all the money I needed to go support my man. I was working at Chene Park again for the summer. So, getting the money was quick and easy. I went with his sister and my girl Desha. I had always wanted to go to New York before Antjuan went on Making the Band, but it was only because I liked how it looked on TV. I never really had a specific reason to go until he went. I tried to come to New York the entire season, but every time it was time for me to come, Diddy would send them home. I couldn't complain when he came home because he would stay longer than I would have been able to visit anyway. So, it worked out for the better.

When we arrived in New York, we couldn't meet up with him immediately. We had to wait until he was available to see us. We met up with him later that night at a bar that was attached to the hotel they were staying at called, The Muse. When we were approaching the bar, I saw the camera crew standing outside taping and waiting for us to arrive. I had given myself a pep talk before I left my hotel to not argue with Antjuan, because I had already done that on the show. However, what they showed on TV wasn't how it happened at all. They tried to make it seem like I had broke up with Antjuan because he didn't have time for me, and Lord knows that wasn't the case at all. While we were in the bar, I noticed Antjuan had an attitude, but I didn't really understand why. Then, it clicked to me. He was upset because he had just told me that he was opening up for New Edition the next day, and I didn't sound as excited as he expected me to be. I was very excited. However, I was use to Antjuan doing big shit. I was real laid back about it, and he took it as me being careless. We exchanged a couple of words, and the cameras were all in. I didn't want to be known as the girl that can't stop arguing with her man. So, I bit my tongue, and decided to just drop it.

Since my girl Desha had to go back to Detroit to her son the next day, we weren't able to stay for the concert. So, I had to wait for him to call me and tell me the results. When he called me later that night, he told me that Diddy didn't even pick the band. Right when they thought he was about to, he got up and walked out of the room and never returned. At first I was a little upset that he was playing with them like that, but then I tried to put myself in Diddy's shoes. He had a lot of talent. It was probably too hard for him to cut anybody. I understood that. He probably just needed some more time. He ended up sending them back home until he was ready, and this time America was going to help decide who would be the next members of the band.

When Antjuan went back to New York, so did I. This time I went with an entourage. It was me, his mother, his cousin Jassyka, my friend Diedra, his manager Ian, his assistant manager Twist, Deandre, Deandre's manager Chris, his friend Nugget, Nugget's son, Twist's girlfriend Tia, his friend Dubbz, my friend Ashley, his aunt Tina, and I am sure I might be missing some more people. Antjuan had no idea that all of us were coming. I had wanted it to be a surprise. When he saw that all of us came out there to support him, he was overjoyed. However, he had to break the news to us that Diddy still wasn't making the band. We were upset that we had come all the way out there and he still wasn't making the band, but we made the best out of our trip. We partied the entire time we were there.

The day that they were suppose to show the finale on TV, they had a little announcement at the end by Diddy telling everyone that he was going to do the finale live on August 26th. I knew then that games were over. He was ready to make the band. It didn't say where the finale would be. So, I had my girl Diedra get on the internet and do some searching, and she found a contact number to the guy that was giving away tickets. I called the guy and left him a message telling him who I was, and telling him that I would appreciate it if he could accommodate me and a couple of my friends. He returned my call a couple of days later, and told me that he would try to get me some tickets, but they had given all the tickets they were going to give away. He said that he would try to at least get me two, because I was June, Robert's girlfriend.

Getting everything together for the finale trip drove me crazy. I had people backing out every five minutes. I even had people trying to stop me from going. All types of obstacles were trying to prevent from going, but I didn't let anything stop me from seeing my baby make the band. My friends and I rented a truck, and we were on our way. There were a lot of people that went to support Antjuan this time. It was way more that came to support Antjuan this time. I can't even remember how many people went. I just knew it was over twenty of us. The day of the finale, my friend Diedra spoke to the guy that told us that he would let me know if I could receive some tickets. When he called us, he told us to give him a call because he had me some tickets. I called him back, and he told me that he couldn't give everyone that I had a ticket, but he had at least two. When he told me that he had two tickets, I knew that it would only be fair to give to Diedra because she had worked so hard to get them for me. I knew that there was going to be some people that were upset because they couldn't get in, but I figured they would get over it. If they couldn't understand why they couldn't get in, it was only because they were being selfish.

When we got in to the studio, the guy that gave me the tickets sat us directly in the front. I honestly didn't think that since it was so last minute, I could get such good seats, but he looked out for us. Once again, he told me that the only reason why he was doing it was because I was who I was. While I was there I had people coming up to me asking me was I June from the show. I was actually kind of flattered because they treated me like I was a celebrity. I had people taking pictures of me, asking for my autograph, and treating me like I was someone they looked up to. All I did was have an argument with the boy. I didn't understand why they thought I was so important. I couldn't complain though.

When the show was about to begin, Young Joc had to do a sound check for his performance. I had notice that he was eying me, but I just figured he was doing it because that's what artist do. I didn't think that it wasn't anything more than that. The people that were running the show told us that we had to be extra hyped when he performed, but I tried to act really reserved because I didn't want Antjuan to think that I was so excited over Young Joc. I liked his music, but I had never been the type to be all over an artist because of who they were. When he performed, he came up to me and grabbed my hand and rapped to me. Any other woman would have probably been excited, but I was scared to death because Antjuan was looking right at me. I should have known that he was going to do that from the way he was looking at me before he actually did his performance. It was nothing though. Antjuan did that to girls all the time. So, I knew he knew it was just a part of his show.

When the boys sang *Exclusive* as a ballad, I felt like I had fell in love with Antjuan all over again. When he sang I felt chills running all though my body, and instantly I began to think of the things I wanted to do him once the show was over. He looked so damn good to me. I felt like a fan that had never seen him a day in my life, and I had to have him. After they sung *Exclusive*, Diddy had cut the boys down to eight people, and the time had come for him to make the band. I had to be as nervous as they were. I knew that Diddy loved Antjuan, he made that very obvious from watching the show. So, I knew that he was going to either make him a solo artist or put him in the band. I was just ready to hear him say it himself. The suspense was killing me.

At first he called the boys up one by one and made them stand in this line as if he were trying to make a decision of he wanted to be in the band. However, he didn't call Antjuan's name one time. He called everyone but him. He wasn't fooling me though. When it was time to make the band, Antjuan was the first name he called. When he said his name, I instantly jumped out of my seat screaming and crying because I was so overjoyed. I knew the moment Antjuan tried out that it was a wrap, but it was now official. Antjuan was signed to Bad Boy.

Chapter 22
Prison

After Antjuan made the band, Diddy sent everyone back home until it was time to go back and start taping Season 2. Things between us had started to get very hectic. We had been arguing damn near everyday. We both had a lot of insecurities, and it was beginning to destroy our relationship. We found ourselves getting mad at things that the average person wouldn't get mad at, and blaming each other for what we knew we were responsible for. One day, after Antjuan and I had a pointless argument, he decided that it was best that we have some time apart.

"What do mean, we need some time apart?" I asked.

"It's not working out June. All we do is argue! I think we need some time to get our shit together, and once we do that everything should be cool. This isn't goodbye."

I honestly didn't think that he was making the best decision. The problems that we had could have been easily prevented, but it seemed like neither one of us could put our pride aside to fix the problem.

During our break up, I noticed that there was something different about Antjuan. Although we spent time together as if we were still a couple, I knew that he may be also talking to other females. I couldn't really grasp the fact that he was a single man again after being with him for so long though. I thought that the purpose of our break up was to make things better, not to make it worse. I knew that I wasn't going to be able to handle him talking to other women. So, I tried to do everything in my power to make him get back with me. However, every time I thought about him and another woman, I would get all emotional and tell him that I didn't want him anymore. I knew in my heart, that's not really what I wanted.

Before I knew it, months had gone by and Antjuan and I were still not together. This was the longest we had ever been broken up. The longest break up we've ever had lasted about a week, probably less than that. I was beginning to feel like he didn't love me anymore. We still talked everyday, he still did things for me, and we still had sex, but it was far from how it use to be. One day, Antjuan and I had a hotel room, and he had told me that there was no possible way that we could get back together feeling the way he felt. He said that he felt like I had been dishonest with him about some things and his heart couldn't let it go. He told me that if I cared about this relationship, then I would just tell him the truth about whatever I was being dishonest about, and take that weight off his heart.

I had never seen Antjuan look so sincere in my life. I loved him to death, and I was tired of us not being together. I was even more tired of having all that weight that I had on my chest. I was far then prepared to tell him what I had in store for him.

"Okay…here it goes. I have cheated on you, other than the time I cheated on you with Antonio. Even though we weren't together at the time of the Antonio incident, I know you still count that as cheating. After the Ryana incident, I had sex with an ex-partner of mine. I even had sex with Antonio again after I got caught the first time. I did that after you did what you did, of course. You were driving me crazy with all of that Shanda and Natasha shit. Don't get it twisted though. I didn't have sex with them consistently. I can count on one hand how many times it happened."

I knew that once I told him, my slate would be clean. I had explained to him that my reasons for doing what I had done were because he was cheating on me, and it drove me to be vindictive. As I was telling him all of this, I could see the pain building up in his eyes. For once, he felt what I felt. He began to see images of me having sex with someone else, and it killed him. I never wanted to hurt him like that. I never wanted to hurt myself like that, but I couldn't take it back. I knew that it wasn't going to be as easy as Antjuan said it was going to be. I knew that he was hurt and he needed time to heal, but I was too scared to give it to him. I felt the moment I let him out of my sight, he would go try to get back at me for what I had done. That would have only made the situation worse. I needed Antjuan to understand that I didn't have sex with someone else because I wanted to. I did it because I was hurt. As silly as it may have sounded, it was the truth. Antjuan stayed with me for at least five days in a row after I told what I had done, and it was the worst experience of my life. His heart had been damaged. I couldn't stand to see him that way. We could hardly have sex because he kept picturing me with someone else. I knew exactly what he was going through. I tried to have sympathy, but every time he described his feelings, I couldn't do anything but relate. I had been experiencing that feeling that he was feeling off and on the entire time we were together.

When we finally separated from each other, he went into the studio and recorded the saddest song that I had ever heard in my life. It was entitled, "Prison". It described everything that he had been going through after I told him what I had done. It hurt me to hear it. I didn't want everyone to know what I had told him, but I should have known that he was going to write a song about it exposing it to the world. His music was nothing but a soundtrack to his life. I had written a ton of poetry about how I felt about Antjuan, both good and bad. So, I couldn't really be too mad.

I tried to explain to Antjuan that I truly did love him, and I was truly sorry for what I had done to him. I didn't want him to think that I was still doing anything outside of him while we weren't together, because I wasn't. I had made a promise to God and myself that I would never hurt him or disrespect myself like that again after the last time I had sex with somebody else. God showed me that being vindictive was far from the answer. It would only complicate things.

Before I knew it, it was September 2007, and Antjuan and I were still not together. We were still trying to fight through the storm. We still loved each other, we still dated, but we were at a stand still. I just decided to put it in God's hands to see what the future may hold for us. The devil is always busy and working against us. Will we be able to beat him? I guess we can, because in the bible it says, "I can do all things through Christ who strengthens me."

You know it's funny how people want to get closer to God when something tragic happens in their life. I hate to put myself in that category of people; however, it is what it is. I have never prayed so hard, and I have never cried so loud until now. I feel weak because I am very aware of what's going on, but God has been the only one getting me through the storm. This experience has most definitely been the most complicated experience I have ever had in my life; but I will not get discouraged. God wouldn't put me through anything that I couldn't overcome. And you know what... *This Girl will always love the boy in the band.*

Tough Love

I never knew....
Love can make you feel so sad...
Make you feel so bad...
That you wish you never had it.
I thought when I was ready to commit,
Everything would be legit,
But that was all BULLSHIT.
Everything was good when we first got together,
Then came the stormy weather, now we both like
WHATEVER...
However, neither one of us can say bye...
Instead we cry...
Wondering why...

We don't just try...
To not let our love die.
But neither one of us wanna make the first move.
What are we tryna prove?
Who really loves who?
Cause if that's the case, I know I really love you.
I just can't handle you doing what you do,
Screwin who you...
Hangin with you crew.
I know it's hard but baby, can you see my point of view?
Do you really have a clue,
What I've been going through?
Sometimes I wish that I was dead, and it's all because of YOU.
I know you love me.
I just guess it's just hard to let it show...
But you need to do something before I just let it go...
If you think we're moving too fast then baby just take it slow...
Fight off them demons that we have and baby just let it flow...
If we just put it in God's hands, he will continue to let us grow.
Ya know???????????

To be continued...

Printed in the United States
212753BV00001B/44/P